D1068057

Hist. Fiction
Erickson

Erickson, Lois N.
Zipporah/Huldah

00000660

DATE LOANED	BORROWER'S NAME	DATE RETURNED
3/30	V Talsm	4/6

Hist. Fiction
Erickson

00000660

Erickson, Lois N.
Zipporah/Huldah

GUIDEPOSTS

Zipporah

Lois N. Erickson

CARMEL • NEW YORK 10512

Erickson, Lois Nordling, 1920-
    Zipporah.
    1. Zipporah.   I. Title.
        221.924

ISBN 0-8280-0518-4

Chapter 1

The clear notes of a flute drifted to Zipporah through the desert air. She couldn't see the player but she knew it was her sister Misha. Only Tarfah and Jamila —two younger sisters—were within sight, resting together in the shade of a boulder, watching the sheep in their care.

Zipporah lifted her own reed flute from her lap and raised it to her lips. Pausing in her song, she listened for answering notes. They came—a signal that all was well with Misha and the three littlest sisters—Tuema, Duhiya, and Fara.

Tucking an escaping strand of her long black hair under her red and yellow headcloth, Zipporah settled back against the side of the hill. Comfortably relaxed, she smoothed her tan camel-hair robe and surveyed the grazing sheep. Behind them, hills stretched away into the shimmering heat and behind them red granite mountains rose, range after range, in majestic splendor. She loved this territory of her tribe. It consisted of hills and valleys for grazing as well as the bare, wild mountains. In the distance she could see stately Mount Horeb with its high, twin peaks.

5

ZIPPORAH

Her thoughts turned to the tribal camp and to a certain young man who had smiled at her this morning before she led her father's flock to the hillside. Thinking of him, she shivered in happy anticipation that soon her father might say, "I've betrothed you to Azaz."

Three sharp notes from Misha's flute broke into her daydreams. A pause. Then three more notes. The danger signal! Some of the sheep raised their heads and stared inquiringly. Quickly Zipporah motioned to Tarfah and Jamila, indicating—as she had taught them—to hide behind a pile of rocks. She laid her hand on her weapon—a smooth, curved throwstick that she always kept within reach. Then she crawled up the hill and peered over the top.

Fara, Tuema, and Duhiya had already disappeared from sight. Crouching in the cleft of a rock, Misha pointed to the rise of another hill. Five camels showed dark silhouettes against the blue sky. Many more appeared—some with riders, some with packs—and below them a large flock of sheep surged across the curve of the hill.

Invading shepherds! From their striped head cloths, Zipporah recognized them as the same men who had raided her tribe's territory the summer before. She lay on the ground, her slender body pressed against the rocky soil. Remembering that grim day, she covered her face with her trembling hands. Never would she forget the sudden appearance of two strange men from behind a boulder near the well, and then the screams from Tarfah and Jamila when the men grabbed them. Instantly she had slung her throwstick and it smashed into one man's head. As he fell to the ground, he released Tarfah. The other man let go of Jamila and dashed away.

Leaving the sheep at the well, the girls had run up the hill to their father's tent. In a few minutes the war cry, "Kill them, kill them" resounded throughout the camp. Mounted on camels, men armed with spears rode swiftly out to avenge the attack. One of her cousins never returned. Later she saw where his brothers had buried him in the sand with stones piled high over the grave to protect it from desert scavagers.

But the invaders hadn't given up. They returned and tried to take over the well. Again the tribal men drove them away. Now the long line of their camels paraded across the hill and the sheep swarmed around them down into a gorge. At last all the animals disappeared from sight.

Misha climbed to the top of the ridge and dropped down next to her sister. "Do you think they'll come to the well?"

Trying to control her apprehension, Zipporah sat up and brushed dust from her robe. "I hope not."

"I'm scared," Misha whispered, her dark eyes full of fear. "So am I."

The five girls clambered up the hill and flung themselves against their other sisters. Tears rolled down Tarfah's brown cheeks. "Do you think they'll kidnap us and do things to us?" she sobbed.

"I'll protect you," Zipporah answered although she was quaking inside herself.

Little Fara clung to her. "Can I stay right next to you?"

Looking into the seven-year-old's wide, brown eyes, Zipporah reassured her, "Of course you can. We're all going to stay near each other, and as soon as we get the sheep together, we'll go to Father." Somehow she managed to speak calmly even though her heart still pounded. Silently she reminded herself that as the oldest daughter in the family, she was responsible for her sisters.

Duhiya twisted her finger in her long black hair. "They

looked like they were headed toward Mount Horeb."

Zipporah glanced toward the desolate mountain. "If they trespass that far, they'll have trouble with our leader. Achmaz would fight to the death before he allowed another tribe near our mountain." She turned to Misha. "Bring your part of the flock over to this side of the hill where mine is."

"Why do I have to bring them over?" The girl's black eyes flashed defiance. "You do it."

Rising to her feet, Zipporah crossed her arms and confronted her sister. "Just because you've turned 18 years old and are just as tall as I am, that doesn't mean you can give orders. I'm still two years older than you."

"I can give orders too."

"No you can't," Zipporah insisted although her voice softened. "You know that Father gave me the responsibility and told me to make all the decisions."

"All right, I'll bring them," Misha grumbled, glancing away. As she walked toward the flock, she picked up a lamb. Then "Haya, haya," she called as she led the sheep over the ridge to join the others. Carrying rods in case the sheep might stray, the sisters took their places alongside the animals.

Zipporah placed her flute into a carrying pouch. With it over her shoulder along with her water pouch, she cradled her throwstick in her left arm. "Keep your stick handy," she reminded Misha.

Holding Fara's hand and picking her way down the stony slope of the hill, she led the flock. A sudden movement from behind a rock caused Zipporah to grab her sister and jump back. It was only a small gray jaboa, leaping away on its long hind legs.

Ordinarily the rodent would not have startled her, but after sighting the invading tribe and their large number of camels, she had reacted with instinctive caution.

"Do we have to go down to the well?" Fara's frightened voice begged for an answer.

"There's no other way to the camp, but you stay here with the flock while I make sure it's safe to go down the trail." Cautiously she advanced and studied the wadi, the dry river bed that lay below. Nothing moved there nor in the ravine leading into it. She surveyed the scene, glancing repeatedly at the sloping banks, the pebbly bottom, and on until the dry river turned and vanished from sight. Clearly visible, the open well was a dark hole at the side of the wadi. Near it troughs, chiseled out of stone, waited for water.

Her gaze shifted from the well and traveled up the opposite bank. There she could see her tribe's low, black goat-hair tents sprawled across the broad-topped crest of a hill. She could make out her father's tent with its space at one end for her and her sisters, the other end reserved for him and her brother Hobab. The center area was open to the front and back.

Just down to the wadi, up the other side to the camp, then she and her sisters would reach safety. "Lord, the God of our people," she prayed, "take us unharmed to our father's tent." She motioned for the others to bring the flock.

Once the trail neared the well, she could no longer see the camp. "We'll have a hard time getting these sheep past the troughs," she told Fara, "but we can't stop to draw water now."

Suddenly Tarfah screamed. From the mouth of the ravine, four men raced toward the well. Jamila shrieked in terror and fell to her knees behind the sheep. Duhiya, Tuema, and Tarfah scurried to hide behind a clump of thorn bushes. Zipporah and Misha pulled Fara to a boulder and pushed her behind it. Then they turned to face the invaders, but ready to jump behind the large rock for protection in case the men slung stones at them.

The invaders advanced. Their short shepherds' cloaks revealed the strong, muscular calves of their legs. Eyeing the sticks in the hands of the young women, they halted near the milling sheep.

"Ai," the largest man shouted. "The daughters of Jethro have come to water their father's sheep at the well. We know who you are, remembering you from last summer." As he took a step closer, Zipporah and Misha shrank toward the boulder. His laugh was harsh. "Go ahead and water your sheep today. Let them drink their fill because this is your last chance. Tomorrow our tribe takes over this watering place."

The four men backed away, then sprinted toward the ravine. Behind the boulder, Fara started to cry.

With her arm around the littlest sister, Zipporah called to the sheep. Restless and confused with no water to drink, they raised their heads and pressed forward, responding to the familiar voice.

Pulling Fara after her, she hurried up the trail toward the camp. The other sisters dashed from their hiding places to herd the flock. Near the top of the path, Fara squealed, "Now that we're near Father's tent, I'm not afraid anymore."

"But I can't slow down," Zipporah replied. "Wait here for Misha while I run ahead to tell Father about the men. Misha," she shouted, "take the flock to the center of the camp. I have to report to Father." Without waiting for a reply, she darted ahead to find him. When she heard the heavy sound of stone on metal, relief spread through her. His figure, sturdy and mature, and his neatly-trimmed gray beard were a welcome sight. He sat in the tent, pounding with his granite mallet on a large copper disk to form it into a bowl.

"Peace, Father," she said breathlessly. Then she blurted, "We saw a tribe arrive from the north. They had lots of camels and a large flock. Four men came to the well and told us that tomorrow the water would belong to them."

"Come," he ordered. "Achmaz should know right away." She followed him to Achmaz' tent. Through the open front she could see the leader's wife leaning over the stones of her hearth, adding dry camel dung to her cooking fire.

"Peace," Jethro greeted her.

The leader's wife straightened up. "Peace."

"I have urgent news for Achmaz."

At the sound of his name, the man emerged from behind a woolen partition that covered the entrance to his section of the tent.

"I am here. What is your message?"

Jethro pushed Zipporah forward. "Tell him." She clasped her hands tightly together and related what had happened at the well.

Folding his arms across his chest, the tribal chieftain let out a loud laugh. "Idle words. Empty threats. That tribe wouldn't dare take over our water supply. We're too strong for them and they know it. Tomorrow you will lead your sheep to graze as usual." He raised his right hand, the sign of dismissal.

Zipporah walked behind her father's straight, proudly-erect figure to his tent. Once inside he drew his hand over his eyes and down onto his beard. "Achmaz is our leader. We must follow his order, but I will make sure that some of my brother's sons take their sheep to graze near mine tomorrow. Those young men can watch for invaders and send someone to tell us if they return again."

ZIPPORAH

Misha appeared with twigs to start the cooking fire. Zipporah added camel dung. Soon bright orange flames danced inside the ring of stones and smoke drifted through a hole in the tent's roof.

After she served the evening meal to her father and brother and after all the sisters had eaten, Zipporah stood outside in the cold night air. She shivered. Even if her cousins came with their sheep, the thought of returning to the grazing place sent a feeling of dread through her.

"Good evening, beautiful daughter of Jethro." The deep voice and a hand on her shoulder brought a smile to her lips. She turned to look up into Azaz' dark eyes. In the fading daylight she was aware of his strong arms where they showed beneath his brown robe. Even more than his arms or his handsome face, she admired his capable hands . . . hands that could fashion turquoise necklaces from the raw stone, polish malachite until veins in the green gem came to life, twist thin strands of silver into exquisite chains. No man in the tribe equaled Azaz in working with metal and stone.

His eyes appraised her smooth face and the sweep of her long black eyelashes. "I heard that you had trouble at the well today," he said. "If any man ever harms you, he'll have to face me."

Her heart fluttered and she yearned for his strong arms around her, never to let go. Embarrassed that she would have such a thought, she dropped her gaze to his goatskin sandals. "Thank you," she managed to say.

"Daughter!" She heard the disapproval in her father's voice. "Who is talking to you?"

"It is I, Azaz," the young man announced.

Jethro appeared at the opening to the tent. "If you wish to visit my family, you may sit with me at my fire, but no daughter of mine will talk or walk with a man in the night."

ZIPPORAH

"My apology. I will return another time." Azaz strode toward his father's tent.

"You will have no secret meetings with this man," Jethro informed Zipporah. "Come inside."

She left the cold night air and entered the women's end of the tent. A collection of orange and red thickly woven rugs covered the rocky soil. Sheepskins were cozy beds, waiting for the tired girls to sleep. Saddlebags held supplies —dates, wheat, millet, and dried coriander, thyme, and oregano wrapped in linen cloths. A pile of bowls, gourds, and basins were pushed into a corner. The sight of the household items helped to ease the turmoil that her father's words had caused.

Misha had lit oil lamps and now the little girls rolled the rugs and placed them against the back wall. Tarfah and Jamila lifted the tent's side. Imitating the throaty call of a ewe to her lamb, Zipporah spoke softly to the sheep outside, "Brrr, brrr, brrr." Then she sang her evening song.

> "Come, little ones,
> do not go astray.
> Inside the tent
> all night you may stay."

Repeating the coaxing sound, "Brrr, brrr," a few of the ewes crowded into the tent. Lambs followed, each one close to its mother. After Jamila and Tarfah lowered the side of the tent, the sheep stood for a while, burping and coughing as they chewed their cud. At last they lay down, lending their warmth to the sisters as a buffer against the bitter, night cold.

With the sheepskin under her and a woolen blanket over her, Zipporah snuggled against the large ewe that was closest to her. Although the good, warm smell of lanolin and wool usually gave her a feeling of security, now she lay awake in apprehension. *Would the invading shepherds return the next day? Was their threat real or was it, as Achmaz insisted, only idle words?*

The following day while they watched the sheep, all the sisters stayed close together. On another ridge their uncle's sons raised shepherds' rods, signaling that they were ready to protect their cousins at the first sign of danger.

Trying to appear composed in front of the younger girls, Zipporah settled onto a rock. To calm her own uneasiness, she combed Fara's hair, stroking it with loving care and fashioning it into two braids. She held one of the deep brown braids . . . brown like her mother's hair . . . Mother whose life had ebbed away when Fara was born. For a moment Zipporah closed her eyes, attempting to blot out the memory. How well she remembered the midwife struggling to stop the bleeding.

"All of us have black hair like Father's," she mused. "You're the only one with hair like Mother's."

Fara cuddled into her sister's lap. "I wish I had a mother." Zipporah held the little girl close to her heart. The sun crawled across the cloudless sky. In the late afternoon it dipped toward the top of the western mountains. *Maybe this day would end without threat or danger from marauding shepherds.*

"God of our forefathers," she prayed, "keep us safe."

Suddenly she heard Jamila gasp, "There's a man!"

Chapter 2

Hide," Zipporah ordered.

All the sisters crawled up the ridge and disappeared on the other side. The two oldest lay down and peeked over the top. "Keep your head low," Zipporah cautioned. "He's coming this way."

"Look at his funny clothes," Misha whispered. "Look at all those pleats in that cloth hanging down under his short robe."

"And worse than his clothes, he doesn't have a beard. Oh, Misha, he's an Egyptian!"

"And he's big too."

Zipporah bit her lip. "Egyptians never travel alone. There must be some other men with him, maybe a whole army. We just can't see them yet."

"But why would they come here so far from the caravan route?"

The stranger stopped for a moment to gaze at the red granite mountains and at imposing Mount Horeb in the distance. Then, shifting his pack from one shoulder to the other, he continued walking until he entered the ravine that led to the dry wadi.

ZIPPORAH

Staring at the place where he had disappeared, Zipporah whispered, "He's gone toward the well."

From down the ridge she heard Duhiya's trembling voice. "Are some men going to come and grab us?"

Zipporah looked at the five younger sisters, a clutch of dark-haired girls huddled together like frightened birds in a nest. "No. There's only one man."

Misha made a choking sound. "What will we do if he's at the well?"

"We have to water the sheep. They didn't have any yesterday. Go to our cousins and ask them to bring their flock at the same time."

"Why don't you . . ." Misha started to object. Then with a shake of her head, she reluctantly agreed. "I'll go." She scrambled away, and soon returned with her lower lip stuck out in a pout.

"What did they say?"

"They said we ought to know there isn't room to water two flocks at the same time, but they promised to come right after we finish."

"Let's go," Zipporah grumbled. She called to the girls and the sheep. Leading the flock toward the well, she stopped at the top of the sloping trail to scan the territory below, but saw no sign of the man. With her throwstick in the ready position and glancing frequently toward the well, she descended the trail and led the sheep onto the level section at the edge of the dry river. "He could be hiding somewhere," she said quietly to Misha. Tarfah retrieved a large goat-leather bag from its place behind a clump of thorn bushes. The four older sisters took turns drawing water and pouring it into the stone troughs. The sheep pushed ahead to drink.

Without warning, five men dashed from the lower end of

the ravine. "The shepherds" Jamila shrieked.

The flock scattered, the animals tumbling over each other in confused panic. The younger sisters raced for the protection of the thorn bushes. Zipporah and Misha grabbed their throwsticks and ran behind a boulder. Watching from around the end of the big rock, they saw the shepherds retreat up the hill and disappear from sight. Near the watering troughs, they now noticed a broad-shouldered man. He stood solidly, a bronze sword raised in his right hand.

"It's the Egyptian!" Misha exclaimed.

Zipporah held tightly to her weapon. Her eyes widened at the sight of this foreign man and his strange clothes, pleated linen hanging below a travel-stained white robe. Wrapped around his head he wore a cloth that left his sunburned neck and face uncovered.

The man lowered his sword and walked toward the boulder. "Don't be frightened," he said slowly. "I come in peace."

The girls crawled out from behind the thorn bushes, Misha picking up the water bag.

The man eyed the stick in Zipporah's right hand. "You can put your weapon away. I won't harm you."

She glanced from the brown stubble on his face to the ornamented hilt of his sword. "How do I know I can trust you?"

He stepped toward the well. "Give me the bag. I'll draw the water for your sheep."

Misha handed him the water bag and he lowered it into the water.

In a low, barely-controlled voice, Zipporah said, "I don't want this Egyptian to help us."

"But he can draw water twice as fast as we can," her sister

insisted. "Just look at those shoulders and how strong he is."

Zipporah frowned. "I don't trust him. What's he doing here?"

"Who cares right now?" Misha giggled. "As long as he's watering the sheep, I'm not going to object."

"You shouldn't talk like that. What if there's a whole army of his people around here somewhere?"

Misha smiled at the man's broad back. "I don't see a whole army—only one handsome Egyptian." She giggled again. "He's even better-looking than Azaz."

Zipporah let out her breath in exasperation. "No man is better-looking than Azaz." Standing well away from the stranger, she looked for her cousins but they were nowhere in sight. When the sheep had drunk their fill, she said to Misha, "You and the girls take the flock up the trail to Father's tent. I'll walk behind to give you protection."

"I don't think that's necessary."

"Do as I say."

Her sister frowned but called for the animals to follow her. As the last animal left the watering troughs, Zipporah bowed slightly to the man. She must thank him. "We are grateful for your effort in drawing water for the flock. May you go in peace and may the Lord bless you." There, she had spoken the correct words. She backed away toward the trail, then turned and hurried to catch up with her six sisters and the flock.

Her father stood outside his tent admiring his flock. "How is it that you have come so soon today?" he asked.

Before she could answer, Duhiya shouted, "Those shepherds came running at us, but an Egyptian scared them away."

Tuema jumped up and down with her right hand in the air.

ZIPPORAH

"He had a sword and he held it up like this."

"He even drew water for us," Misha broke in, "and he watered the flock."

"Where is he?" Jethro demanded. "Why have you left the man down there at the well?" He turned his stern gaze on his two eldest daughters. "Summon him that he may come to my tent and eat bread."

Zipporah cringed. An Egyptian? Ask an Egyptian to eat with her father? For a brief moment she closed her eyes in protest. Then she took a deep breath and opened them. She and Misha must obey their father.

Standing at the top of the trail, Zipporah scanned the wadi below. "I can't see him." Misha glanced anxiously up to the hills. "Maybe he's gone."

"We'd better find him. Let's look by the well first." As quietly as possible they picked their way down the stony path to the flat surface of the wadi. Near the well Misha drew in a sharp breath. "There's someone behind the thorn bushes."

Grasping her sister's arm, Zipporah drew her back. The man they were seeking stepped around the end of the shrubs and advanced toward them. "Peace."

"Peace," they replied.

"Have you lost a lamb?"

Zipporah let go of Misha and then stood straight and proudly in front of him. Did he think she and her sister were so careless they would lose one of their animals? "Of course not. We've come with a message for you from our father, the priest of the Kenite tribe of Midian."

He raised his eyebrows. "A message for me?"

She paused, wishing she did not have to deliver it. Then she stated bluntly, "Our father invites you to his tent to share the evening meal."

19

A pleased look crossed his face before he replied, "I'll get my pack from behind the bushes."

When he reappeared, Zipporah announced, "My sister will lead the way up the trail."

As he followed Misha, he slowed his steps and smiled over his shoulder at the older girl who had dropped slightly behind him. "You still don't trust me, do you?"

His statement deserved no answer. She pressed her lips together and remained silent.

Jethro stood in front of his tent, watching for the return of his daughters. He drew his hand down the length of his beard.

"I should have gone myself," he muttered.

His son Hobab emerged from the tent. "What did you say, Father?"

"What's taking them so long?" the priest grumbled. "That Egyptian was armed with a sword and he could become dangerous."

Hobab pointed to the top edge of the trail. "I see Misha now."

Jethro squinted against the sun, low in the sky. "Where's Zipporah?"

"There she is, right behind the stranger." Jethro breathed deeply. His daughters were safe. Now he straightened his back, waiting to extend hospitality toward the solitary traveler. *Would the Egyptian accept it? Would he eat with a Midianite?*

The stranger halted directly in front of him. "I come in peace."

"Welcome in peace to my humble tent." He led the way through the open front into the center space. Stepping past the stones of the hearth, he lifted a woolen drape. "Do me the honor of entering my room." Bright red and orange rugs covered the ground. An array of metal-working tools spread over one rug, and thick sheepskins covered two camel saddles. Jethro invited the visiter to sit down and lean against a saddle. "We will rest here until my daughters bring water and the evening meal."

Near the cooking fire Zipporah poured water into two striped gourds, placing them—along with a small bowl—into a copper basin.

Little Fara squatted beside her. "Are you ready to wash his feet?"

"I guess I'm ready."

Misha's eager voice startled her. "If you don't want to do it, I will."

"That wouldn't be proper. I'm the oldest and it's my duty."

The younger sister turned away to sulk. "You're just pretending you don't want to wash his feet."

Am I pretending? Zipporah wondered. There was something intriguing about the man even if he was an Egyptian . . . or maybe because he was. Picking up the basin, she stood by the curtain to her father's room. "May this daughter come in?"

"Enter."

Kneeling in front of the guest, she untied his sandal thongs. When her hand brushed against his foot, a strange sensation tingled up her arm. She wanted to look into his face and see the hue of his brown eyes more closely. But no! She mustn't.

Her father nodded his approval as he watched her pour water from a gourd over the man's feet and hands, catching it in the basin. Filling the small bowl with cool water from the other gourd, she offered it for the guest to drink.

Returning to the cooking fire, she supervised the

evening meal preparations. As soon as Farfah brought fresh camel milk, Zipporah took it and sidled into her father's room.

"Set it here," Jethro ordered, pointing to a mat in front of him. Then he turned his attention back to the visitor. "All strangers who come to Midian are the Lord's guests and they share alike with the tribe. Will you who appear to come from Egypt accept my hospitality and break bread with me?"

The man was silent for a moment before he answered, "I am from Egypt and I'm grateful for your hospitality." Raising his hand, Jethro dismissed his daughter from the room.

Misha stirred the boiling wheat porridge. "I get to take something in," she insisted.

"All right. You can take the wheat."

Misha removed the steaming porridge from the fire and topped it with buttermilk. Carrying a bag of salt and a pile of warm flatbread, Zipporah followed her into their father's quarters.

Jethro placed the pot of wheat close to his guest and indicated that he should tear pieces off the bread and dip them into salt and then the hot meal.

The man nodded and started to eat.

With well-salted bread Jethro too scooped hot wheat into his mouth. "With this salt and bread we have made a covenant. As long as food we eat together remains in your belly, you have safe passage anywhere within our tribal territory."

"I am thankful."

Listening outside the drape, Zipporah and Misha heard their father say, "Now I will tell you my name. I am Jethro, priest of the Kenite tribe of Midian. We are metal workers and herdsmen. My son Hobab takes care of my camels, and my daughters watch the sheep."

The stranger paused before replying slowly. "I am Moses from Egypt." Then the sisters heard their father's customary words of hospitality, "My tent is your tent."

The man's answer, low and guarded, came indistinctly through the partition. Their father's voice replied in little more than a whisper. Misha's eyes gleamed brightly. "What do you think he's telling Father?"

Chapter 3

The following morning Zipporah and Misha sat near the top of a rocky hillside, watching the sheep below them graze slowly up the slope. Misha glanced in the direction of the camp. "I'd still like to know what that Egyptian was telling Father."

Zipporah frowned. "I'm sure it was something he didn't want us to hear."

"What do you think of him?"

"I don't know. What am I supposed to think?"

The younger sister's voice rose in excitement. "You can't help but notice how handsome he is."

"I've noticed."

Misha raised her eyebrows. "Admit it. He's handsomer than Azaz."

"I only admit that he's taller than Azaz."

Tarfah's shout broke into the argument. "Father is coming with that other man."

The stranger now wore one of Jethro's robes. Over his head he wore a white Midianite-style headdress, held in place with black goat-hair cords. It hung to his shoulders and only partially concealed his short hair.

ZIPPORAH

"Daughter," Jethro called to Zipporah. She scrambled down the hillside to stand in front of him. "My flock has increased. I've come to divide it," he informed her. "Moses will take half of the sheep to graze near your cousins."

With the man so physically close, it was difficult to concentrate on her father's words, yet she managed to hear him say, "Tell Misha and the girls to keep the sheep from straying while I made the division. And you cut a staff for Moses."

"Yes, Father." She cringed at the thought of a weapon in the stranger's hands, but her father had ordered it. "I'll get my knife so I can cut a branch from an acacia tree."

Moses led the way to a tree. "Your father said a rod with a knob on the end is best for beating off wild animals." He reached for her knife. "I'll cut it."

Wanting to insist that she was capable of doing it, she hesitated before reluctantly handing the knife to him. He lopped off a straight branch with a round knob and gave the knife back to her. "Through your father's hospitality, the Lord is blessing me with a place to live and work to do."

"How do you know about our God?"

He gazed at a distant hill. "Egypt has temples for many gods, but years ago my sister Miriam told me about the one true God."

Zipporah frowned in unbelief. "How would an Egyptian woman know about the God of heaven?"

"Miriam is not Egyptian. She's Hebrew, as I am."

Eyeing him doubtfully, she dared to ask, "If you're Hebrew, why have you cut your beard like the Egyptians?"

"It's a long story and I'll tell you some day."

She glanced down at a thorn bush that grew near a pile of rocks. "Shall we go back to the sheep now?" As soon as they had divided the flock, Jethro and Moses led half of the sheep to another hillside.

Misha sighed."I hope he's not going back to Egypt for a long, long time."

Shrugging her shoulders, Zipporah remarked, "It was more peaceful before he came."

"I don't need it peaceful when it could be more exciting."

"Don't talk like that!"

"Do you think he'll want to take a wife?" The younger sister's voice betrayed her hope.

"Maybe. But no woman in our tribe would want to marry a foreigner."

"I would if that foreigner was Moses."

"Misha!"

Throughout the day she caught herself staring at the man on the other hillside. The sight of him drew her, but each time she looked quickly away, hoping Misha hadn't noticed her fascination with the stranger.

Later after the evening meal in her father's tent, she headed for the center of the camp where shepherds and herdsmen watched over the tribe's sheep, goats, camels, and donkeys during the night.

She soon found her brother Hobab sitting on a rug and leaning against the side of his camel. His brown dog rushed to meet her, wiggling a friendly welcome. About the size of a half-grown lamb, the animal's tail curved over its back and now wagged vigorously. Zipporah stooped down to rub the dog behind its ears.

As she walked toward Hobab, he smiled and moved to make room for her on the rug.

"First I want to comb Tala," she said, glancing around for the camel. On her fifteenth birthday her father had presented her with a baby camel and she had immediately loved it. With all the petting and grooming during the last five years, she felt sure Tala loved her too—at least the creature never spit at her or tried to bite.

"She's right there behind Father's riding camel," Hobab replied.

As she approached the animal, Zipporah sang softly. Then Tala allowed her to stroke her neck and comb dirt from her coat. The tan hair shone golden in the rays of the setting sun. When the camel nuzzled against her waistband, Zipporah laughed and pulled out the dried dates that she had brought for a treat.

Satisfied with the grooming, she returned to sit with her brother. His dog lay down beside her and absently she stroked its back.

"You're very quiet," he observed. "Is something the matter?"

"Yes," she admitted, knowing she could trust him with her innermost thoughts. "Misha is becoming restless."

"In what way?"

"She says silly things about that foreigner." Then she whispered, "Father should have found husbands for Misha and me long ago. I know he wants to keep us so we can watch his sheep, but we're already so old. Who's going to want us?"

Hobab nodded. "Do you want me to speak to Father about this?"

"Oh yes, please do."

"And is there someone special you want me to mention to Father for you?"

Zipporah giggled.

"For example," he continued, "my friend Azaz?"

She laughed again. "Maybe."

27

ZIPPORAH

"I saw Father and Azaz' father talking together just a couple of days ago."

"Did you really?"

"Of course. You know I wouldn't lie to you."

The sun had slipped behind the western mountains. She stood up. "I have to go now and call some sheep into the tent. Don't forget to talk to Father."

"I won't forget."

The next afternoon when she returned from the well, Zipporah saw Hobab standing at the top of the trail. She fell into step with him and waited for him to speak.

"I mentioned to Father that you and Misha are past marrying age," he reported.

"What did he say?"

"All he said was that he would decide when and whom you will marry."

The moon waxed and waned through its monthly cycle and cold winds blew down from the north. Many mornings frost embroidered the ground. Bunches of grass turned brown and the sheep grew restless when even that dry food became scarce. Achmaz called the tribal men together and announced, "Before the second rising of the sun, we will travel south."

"So be it," the men responded.

The morning of the migration, Hobab brought camels for his sisters to load—one camel for the tent and others for the large saddlebags filled with grain and dates, bowls and grinding stones, blankets and cushions. Zipporah and Misha threw sheepskins, rugs, and rods for a loom across the top of the loads, securing them with palm-fiber ropes. The donkeys carried tan goatskins of water, slung crossways under their bellies.

ZIPPORAH

Achmaz mounted his riding camel. Shouting, "Wolloo, wolloo," he signaled for the people to ride after him.

Zipporah rubbed Tala's neck before she settled herself on the shaggy animal's back. Mounting behind her, Fara clung to her sister's robe. Then, gurgling and sucking as it chewed its cud, the camel plodded along on smooth padded feet. Around and among the camels, sheep and donkeys followed the caravan with guard dogs to keep them from straying and tribal goats leading the way.

Early morning sunshine touched the mountain ranges, turning the red granite into an explosion of color—green, yellow, orange.

Zipporah never tired of the mountains' beauty, their ever-changing hues and majestic heights. The migration south was her favorite. She loved the trek through a maze of deep wadis and then the breeze that brought a damp smell from the turbulent sea.

As the day warmed, she pulled her shawl forward to shade her eyes, and retrieving her flute from a saddlebag, she played a wandering melody to encourage the sheep and camels on the journey. Ahead of her Moses and her father rode side by side. She looked past them, searching for a glimpse of Azaz.

Late in the afternoon Achmaz sent up a shout to announce that he had sighted the oasis where they would camp for the night. Other riders echoed the call until it reached the end of the caravan.

Raising their heads in anticipation, the goats and sheep hurried forward. Date palms ringed a pond of water. Zipporah urged Tala along with the heel of her bare foot. She halted the camel at the edge of the oasis and with her hand on its neck, whistled for the creature to kneel. Pausing only to tie on her sandals, she slipped off the camel and immediately looked for stones that would mark a previous traveler's cooking fire. Soon the comforting smell of boiling barley soup, flavored with coriander, came from the pot on her fire.

She was mixing wheat flour and water for flat bread to bake on hot stones when she heard a sudden cry from Fara. Sobbing, the little girl rushed into her arms. "I fell down and cut my hand on a sharp rock." Zipporah stared in horror at the blood oozing from the gash. As always, the sight of blood brought a vision of her dying mother. She slumped to the ground, screaming, "Jamila, come help me."

Jamila wiped Fara's hand and glanced at Zipporah. "It's only a little cut. Why are you always so scared?"

Zipporah shook her head. "I'll just sit here for a few minutes." She waited until the dizziness subsided before returning to the cooking fire.

Slowly recovering from her fright, she noticed a band of Ishmaelite traders pitching their tents and spreading out their wares on the opposite side of the oasis.

"Watch the soup," she instructed Jamila. "Stay right here and don't let it burn. I'm going over to the Ishmaelites to see if they have any wheat to sell."

A deep voice behind her offered, "I'll go with you to carry the grain."

She glanced behind her. Finding Moses suddenly so close, she faltered, "That's not necessary. I can take a donkey."

"I'm as strong as a donkey," he insisted. She saw laughter reflected in his brown eyes.

"Of course." It was inappropriate to refuse when a man offered help. Her heart beat faster. Although he had lived in her father's tent for many moons, she had never walked alone with him. Picking up a saddlebag and a copper bowl, she glanced across the oasis. "I'm ready to go."

At the Ishmaelite camp she examined grain in a basket, lifting handfuls to inspect the wheat kernels. The Ishmaelite scrutinized her copper bowl before he started a lively haggling for the amount of grain he was willing to give in exchange for it. After they reached agreement, he poured wheat into the saddlebag.

Moses picked it up and slung it over his shoulder. Carrying the heavy bag easily, he said, "I've never bargained for grain. Of course I lived in Egypt where the household slaves always took care of buying."

"You mean your household had slaves?"

He nodded and she glanced more carefully at him. His dark brown beard had grown thick. With it and the Midianite robe he was wearing, he could pass as a man of her tribe or as a Hebrew—except that he didn't look like a poor slave worker. He bore himself like the commander of an army. Something about his straight back and the proud lift of his head led her to ask, "If you lived in a household that had slaves, why have you come to Midian?"

He laughed. "Women shouldn't ask questions like that." Then he was suddenly serious. "Hasn't your father told you why I left Egypt?"

Chapter 4

I know only what you've told me—that you are Hebrew." She waited eagerly to hear his reason for leaving Egypt. *Was that what he had whispered to her father when he had first arrived many moons before?*

Moses shifted the saddlebag to his other shoulder and walked closer to her. "Let me explain why I lived in a household with slaves. When I was three months old, Pharaoh's daughter adopted me. Until I came to Midian, I lived in a palace."

He isn't going to tell me why he left, she realized in disappointment. *And can I really believe that he lived in the Egyptian king's palace? Of course he acts like royalty and I've heard some of the tales he's told my father. . . stories of the great Pharaoh and of a vast temple for Ra, the one they called the sun god.*

He set the bag of wheat down near her cooking fire. "I met secretly with my Hebrew family."

"Is that when your sister Miriam told you about the Lord God of heaven?"

"Yes, and my brother Aaron said that more than four hundred years ago, the Lord promised the land of Canaan to the descendants of Abraham's son Isaac. My people are strong and rebellious, but they need to choose a leader. Then the Lord will take them out of slavery."

"He could give them a leader," she declared.

Moses glanced at her, strange emotions flickering across his face. "When? Why is the God of both of our peoples waiting?" he exploded.

She recoiled from his outburst. "The Lord knows why," she replied softly. "My father says that if we listen to His voice, we will understand His plans for us."

"Listen and understand," Moses muttered.

Zipporah watched him walk toward the sheep. *Why would a man raised as a prince choose to live in a Midianite tent when he was accustomed to a palace?* Shaking her head, she turned her attention to the barley soup.

Before dawn the caravan journeyed on. Swaying along on their camels, the tribe ate a midmorning meal of bread and dates. By late afternoon Achmaz raised his hand high. The sea lay a day's journey away but for now the tribe would camp in a valley where a reliable spring flowed from the side of a mountain to form a pool. Stunted date palms ringed the water.

While the sisters prepared the evening meal, Misha fretted. "All Father does is listen to Moses talk about Egypt. I wish he would take time to find husbands for us."

Zipporah glanced toward her father and the foreigner who were in deep conversation. "Even Tarfah and Jamila should be promised in marriage," she said. "Father will have to do something about us soon."

After the evening meal the two men sat comfortably by the fire. "You are silent," Jethro remarked.

"I have something on my mind." Moses hesitated briefly. "In Egypt I took no wife. I wanted a woman who worshiped the Lord, but I wouldn't bring a Hebrew slave into the palace as my wife. So I have waited, trusting that our God would find the right one for me at the proper time."

"And now you are in Midian," the older man prompted.

"For awhile I will stay here."

Long before this evening Jethro had considered the possibility that Moses with his strength and intelligence would make a good son-in-law. "I have seven daughters," he remarked.

"In Pharaoh's court I learned something not only of your language but also of your law. I know a man must pay a bride-price. There is enough silver and gold in my pack."

Following the customary tradition of bargaining, Jethro shrugged his shoulders and replied, "What does silver or gold matter to me? Which of my daughters would you want?"

"I wouldn't think of taking Zipporah without paying the bride-price," Moses replied, indicating which of the daughters he preferred.

"My daughter is beautiful."

"I have heard that a father might accept thirty-five *debens* of silver."

Jethro drew his eyebrows together in a frown. "Some fathers might. God forbid that I would!"

"Or even forty."

"My brother accepted forty-five *debens* of silver as a bride-price for his eldest daughter," the priest suggested.

The younger man put his hand on his chin and stared at the tent's ceiling.

"I brought mainly gold when I came from Egypt, but I can pay you an equivalent value—say fifteen *debens* of gold?"

Jethro paused, hoping he didn't show how pleased he would be to have the Egyptian gold. Then he slowly replied,

"I will accept fifteen *debens* of gold as Zipporah's bride-price."

Moses reached for his pack.

"We can weigh it now."

"Yes, we can weigh it now," agreed Jethro, "and later I will inform my daughter."

Before dawn the morning of the next migration while Zipporah knelt in the tent to pack saddlebags, she heard her father's voice. "Daughter, come out here."

She hurried to him. "Here I am."

"I have something to tell you."

"Yes, Father."

"I have chosen your husband and he has paid your bride-price."

Smiling at him, she waited for the words that would tell her she was promised to Azaz.

"I'm giving you to Moses."

Her eyes blinked and her mouth opened but she made no sound.

"Well, isn't my eldest daughter pleased that I have arranged her marriage?"

Now words tumbled out. "I'm surprised. I always expected to marry a man from our tribe."

"Midianites, Ishmaelites, Hebrews." Her father shrugged his shoulders and lifted his hands. "We're all sons of the sons of Abraham."

Timidly she asked, "Are you sure he's a descendant of Abraham? Maybe he's really an Egyptian."

"Moses says he's Hebrew and I believe him," the priest thundered. "By giving you to this fine man, I'm honoring you."

She stepped back. "Then I will have to weave some material for a new tent."

"You have the usual betrothal time. Be sure you have the tent ready at the end of a year." He strode toward the waiting camels.

Zipporah stood in the semi-darkness, only dimly aware of the pale orange sky to the east. A gentle breeze brought the fragrance of wild lavender. Somewhere a baby cried. They were the familiar smells and sounds that were dear to her. As the bright curve of the rising sun burst over the horizon, she prayed, "Lord, how can I learn to please a foreign prince? And how can I forget Azaz? Help me! I'm too weak to help myself."

When she heard Moses come out of the tent, she started to walk away.

"Wait!" With a quick stride, he stood next to her. "I heard your father tell you of our betrothal."

Determined not to cringe, she looked directly at him.

"At the next camp, I will start to weave a tent."

He laid his warm hand on her arm and spoke kindly. "I hope the news wasn't too much of a shock."

His touch sent a vibration up her arm. "I . . . I just need time to prepare," she stammered. The first rays of sunlight caught the smile in his eyes and on his lips. Standing this close to him, she suddenly wondered what it would feel like to nestle her head against his strong shoulder.

"Zipporah!" Misha's angry voice broke into her thought. "We have to pack."

"I must go," she murmured.

Removing his hand from her arm, he assured her, "When there is more time, we will talk again."

Entering the tent, she could tell by the hunch of her sister's shoulders that she was irritated. "You left me alone with all this packing," Misha complained. "I'm glad you've finished standing out there with Moses." She stuffed a robe into a saddlebag. "What did Father want?"

Zipporah paused a moment before saying, "He wanted to tell me that I'm promised."

"Promised to Azaz at last."

"No, to Moses."

"To Moses!" Misha stood up and confronted her sister, her body quivering with barely suppressed emotion. "You're the lucky one. I wish he'd given me."

An unexpected wave of anger swept over Zipporah. With a shake of her head she tried to fling it away.

Misha's voice was a thick whisper. "I know you want to marry Azaz. Since you don't want Moses, I'm going to ask Father to give me instead of you."

Her sister's words sent a shiver through her. "You can't do that. It's not proper, and besides he's already paid my bride-price."

The younger woman stuck out her lower lip. "Even the day of your wedding, Moses could change his mind and ask for me instead of you."

"Father wouldn't allow it. It's against tradition."

The sister turned away. "It's happened before in our tribe."

All through the day's march, the news of her father's choice whirled in Zipporah's mind. It had never occurred to her that he would promise her to a foreigner. And why would Moses, who probably could marry a princess, want to marry a Midianite woman who lived in a tent? Could she please this man who had spent all his life in a palace with slaves to wait on him? Would he someday come to love her? Could she learn to love him?

Misha's voice jarred into her thoughts. "Before we left camp, I talked to Father."

"You didn't!"

"Yes, I did. He said a woman shouldn't ask questions, and he would make the decision."

"Father has already made the decision," Zipporah insisted while silently trying to ignore the apprehension that nagged at her. "I am promised to Moses." She looked ahead to where he and her father rode side by side on their camels.

Searching for a glimpse of Azaz, she saw him riding next to their tribal chieftain. The man she had hoped to marry aided Achmaz in keeping the caravan moving.

"He's handsomer than Moses, isn't he?" Misha teased.

Zipporah refused to answer her sister's barb. Her gaze returned to Moses. Although Azaz presented a gallant appearance, the foreigner had a regal dignity about him. Again she wondered if she could learn to love this man to whom she was promised. Already she regarded him with . . . what was it . . . respect perhaps . . . but could she, as his wife and as the mother of his children, come to love him?

At the end of the day while she gathered twigs for a fire, she heard steps behind her and then felt a rough pull that brought her to her feet. Azaz' voice was harsh. "I hear you're promised to Moses."

At his sudden statement, Zipporah winced. "Yes, it's true."

"No woman from our tribe should marry an outsider, even if he claims to be a prince."

"My father gave . . ."

"You should not have agreed," he fumed.

She resolved not to submit to his anger. "I will do what my father tells me, not what you think is right or wrong."

As he glared at her, she noticed a cruel glint in his eyes that she had never seen before.

"Well, your man from Egypt can have you. I want a

woman who is loyal to the tribe." He stalked away.

"I am loyal to my tribe," she insisted. "If I disobeyed my father, I would be unworthy." But Azaz was too far away to hear.

Was this the man she had wanted for her husband? With trembling hands she stooped again to pick up firewood.

Using the camels as windbreaks and the sheep for warmth against the sharp night air, the tribe slept without putting up their tents. Zipporah lay awake staring up at the bright stars in the dome of the heavens.

The familiar strong, musky odor of the camels and the smell of their sour breath when they belched surrounded her. She lay next to Tala and stroked the camel's neck. Then, trying to still her restlessness, she cuddled little Fara. Sheep crowded close, coughing and rumbling while they chewed their cud. Nearby her father snored. She wondered if Moses was asleep or was he awake thinking of her while she lay with eyes open, trying to sort out her jumbled thoughts.

The next day Achmaz led the caravan to the sea and along the wide sandy beach in the direction of the copper mines. During the next three moons the tribe turned into narrow valleys, seeking bunch grass, and when it was gone, resuming their journey until they finally arrived at the mines.

Early one morning the men began shearing the sheep. Moses soon learned how to crouch over a ewe or a ram and remove the wool with a bronze knife. While the shearing continued one full moon, the seven sisters helped to keep the animals from straying. Then the men loaded bags of wool onto camels. A short ride took them to the village of the copper miners—to trade wool for metal.

When Zipporah was younger, her father had allowed her

to accompany him to the mines and to see the strange smelting furnaces with their tall chimneys or foot-operated bellows. Now that she was betrothed, it was not proper for her to visit another tribe.

Even before the tribe had finished shearing the last animals, some of the ewes had given birth to lambs. The men set aside their metalworking tools and spent day and night watching the sheep, guarding them against attacks from hyenas and wolves. While the men tended the flocks, Zipporah had extra time to weave strips for her tent.

Fara came often to sit by the loom. One evening she stuck out her lips in a serious pout. "Why aren't you going to marry Azaz?"

The girl's question was one that Zipporah had discarded long ago. Her thoughts and daydreams no longer centered around the man from her tribe. "Father promised me to Moses."

"I thought you wanted to marry Azaz. Don't you want to anymore?"

"I used to think so, but now . . . oh, I just wish my betrothal time would hurry up and end."

Fara's voice was barely more than a whisper. "I guess you like Moses because he's big and strong."

Zipporah stopped weaving for a moment and patted her little sister's hand. "It's hard to explain why a woman likes a man. You'll understand when you're older."

Before the year's betrothal time elapsed, twice more the tribe made long migrations. Then the caravan halted in a valley near Mount Horeb. With the tent pitched, Zipporah set up her loom.

"Are you almost finished with your new tent?" Fara inquired.

"Almost."

ZIPPORAH

"Does that mean you'll have the wedding soon?"

"I have to finish this last strip."

"Most weddings are nice," the little sister said wistfully.

Zipporah had always loved weddings, but now she hunched her shoulders in anxiety.

"You're frowning," Fara observed. "What's the matter?"

"Nothing." Zipporah stared at the shuttle in her hand. *What if the day before or even the day of the wedding itself, Moses would go to her father and say, "Zipporah doesn't please me. I want Misha instead." What if her father answered, "So be it."*

She would be left without the man she had learned to love.

Chapter 5

Fara's pleading voice broke into her thoughts. "Can we look at the wedding dress?"

Zipporah laid aside her shuttle. "Of course." Unfolding a large shawl, she took out a long robe woven from wool.

Fara stroked the soft folds. "Our mother made it, didn't she?"

"Yes, and before she wove it, she used bay leaves to dye the yarn this delicate green. Mother told me that Auntie embroidered the red and orange design around the neck."

Without warning, Fara began to cry. Taking the little girl in her arms, Zipporah rocked her back and forth. "What's the matter?"

"I don't want you to go away," Fara sobbed. "After you marry Moses, I'm afraid he'll take you to that country he came from." She hid her face against her sister's breast. "I always pretend like you're my mother, and if you go away, I won't have a mother anymore."

To comfort the child, Zipporah held her close. To still her own persistent worry, she laid her cheek against the top of Fara's head. *What if Moses did indeed take her to Egypt and she had to live behind the walls of a palace? How could a person breath inside a place that was so enclosed?*

"I wish our mother was still alive," Fara sniffled.

"I do too." Now a deeper-rooted fear shuddered through Zipporah. She had watched their mother's life ebb away. *What if . . . what if she, too, bled to death while giving birth to a child?*

Toward the end of the betrothal year, the finished tent lay folded, ready to set up for the bride and groom.

The night before the wedding, Zipporah tossed restlessly under her blanket. A lamb strayed outside and its mother called loudly to bring it back into the tent. Near her bed Zipporah heard a ram cough. Uneasy sleep finally came until a lamb's sucking awakened her. She could smell the warm milk that overflowed the sides of its mouth. Why didn't daylight come? At last she reached her hand under the wall of the tent and raised it enough to see pale pink sky in the east.

Before her sisters left for the pasture, they clustered around the bride to take her to Auntie's tent. Carrying her wedding robe, Zipporah walked within the circle of excited girls.

During the quiet of the day, she bathed and her aunt rubbed her arms and legs with Damascus rosewater.

"Now you must rest," Auntie ordered.

She felt like shouting, *I don't want to rest. I want this day to end. Then I'll know that I have Moses for my husband.* But dutifully she lay down on the sheepskin as her aunt had ordered. Hours later the sound of shepherds bringing sheep back to the camp alerted her. Her sisters and girl cousins dashed into the tent.

"Wait now," Auntie cautioned. "You must take turns with dressing the bride."

Misha asserted her right as the second oldest daughter.

"I get to put the wedding robe on her."

Zipporah stood up and fingered the softness of the fine wool. She waited while her sister slipped the robe over her head.

"We can do the braids," announced the three cousins. They plaited her long black hair into four braids that hung to her waist.

Auntie handed Tarfah a necklace of turquoise beads. The girl fastened them around Zipporah's neck.

"My turn," Jamila insisted. "What can I do?"

"Here's the veil." Auntie handed a white cloth to the younger sister. It shone with small copper and silver disks, sewn to it in rows. "Tie it on so it covers the lower part of her face." After several tries, Jamila managed to place the veil correctly. The little girls picked up a cream-colored shawl brightly embroidered in red and green, and draped it over the bride's head.

"Oh!" Tuema declared, "you look beautiful."

Zipporah sank down onto a rug and thought, I *hope I look beautiful enough for a man raised in a palace.*

Now the tribal women and girls crowded into the tent to exclaim over the bridal gown, the shawl, the veil. One woman announced, "We've spent all day roasting mutton and making bread. The men are eating now."

Zipporah sighed. The men would take a long time with their leisurely meal. After they finished, the women could eat what was left. While they waited, her guests vied with each other, telling long tales about the birth of their children. Fara fell asleep with her head on the soft fabric in the bride's lap. Barely listening to the women's animated voices, Zipporah forced herself to sit still.

After the sky had darkened, boys came with remnants of the feast . . . half-filled bowls of savory boiled barley and chunks of mutton, flat loaves of wheat bread wrapped around butter-dipped dates.

While the women ate, Zipporah strained to listen for the sound of her brother's voice or the snort of the camel he would bring for her to ride.

Misha threaded her way through the crowded tent to sit on the rug next to the bride. "I'm going to be married," she whispered.

Zipporah clenched her hands into tight fists. No, *not this late on the wedding day! Would her father and Moses make a new agreement even during the feast?* She had heard tales of last minute changes for the women of her tribe.

"Wouldn't you like to know who the man is?" Misha teased.

The muscles in Zipporah's neck tightened into hard knots and her head began to throb. "If you wish to tell me?" she replied with as much dignity as she could manage.

"Shall I wait and let you find out for yourself?"

Drawing her shawl more firmly around her shoulders, Zipporah inhaled deeply and remained silent.

"I might as well tell you that it's Azaz, the man you wish you could marry."

A feeling of relief spread over Zipporah, quickly replaced with anger. "I don't want to marry Azaz," she snapped. "Moses is the one I love."

"You're just pretending you love Moses. I know you still want Azaz."

Suddenly the girls by the door shouted, "He's here," announcing that Hobab had arrived with Jethro's largest camel to take his sister to her groom. Holding tiny clay oil lamps, the sisters escorted Zipporah out of the tent. Her brother helped her onto the camel and it rocked to its feet. While Hobab led the animal slowly toward their father's tent, its decorated saddle swayed on the soft hump, setting bright bells and tassels to swing in rhythm with the camel's gait.

With all the women and girls trailing along, Hobab paraded the bride around Jethro's tent seven times. Each time they passed the front opening, Zipporah peered over her veil, glancing beyond the tribal men to Moses and her father sitting by the fire.

After escorting his sister into the tent she had woven, Hobab left her alone in the darkness. Soon she heard men shouting, "The bridegroom is coming." Her own silent voice questioned, Is *this really happening to me*? The curtain to her room opened and her six sisters entered, each carrying a clay lamp. They nested the lights on a rug. By their reddish-yellow glow Zipporah saw Moses standing in front of her. Acutely aware of his warmth and strength as he untied her veil, she felt him slide his hand down her arm until it touched her fingers. Giggling, her sisters left.

She withdrew her hand. "Now I must prepare the tent." Pulling at a pole until she loosened it from the roof, she allowed a corner of the tent to sag. Outside, the crowd yelled approval and congratulations at this sign that the bride and groom were alone. A few minutes later the noise faded in the distance. Now Zipporah faced her husband. In the lamplight she could see his broad smile.

Gently he drew her to him. Bending his head toward her ear, he whispered, "A year was a long time to wait for this moment with you."

She could smell the pleasant fragrance of frankincense mixed with sesame oil on his beard.

"It was long for me too," she admitted.

With his arm around her waist he led her toward the bed of sheepskins. "When we consummate this marriage, you will become a member of my tribe."

"Your tribe?" she faltered.

"A woman must become a member of her husband's family. That is part of every marriage covenant."

"I am a Midianite, a descendant of Abraham's son Midian," she murmured in protest.

His answer was low.

"And I am a Hebrew, a descendant of Abraham's son Isaac." His arm tightened around her. "But this is no time to talk."

Six moons later Zipporah ran her hand over her belly. Where it should have bulged, it remained flat. Silently she endured her two fears. How could she please her husband without producing sons for him? Yet how could she give birth to a child without dying? More moons brightened and waned. The seasons passed. The tribe migrated. A son was born to Misha and Azaz . . . then another son . . . and a daughter. Tarfah and Jamila married men from the tribe. Women whispered, "Moses' wife has no child. Why isn't the Lord looking on her with favor?"

Duhiya and Tuema married. One day Fara came to her oldest sister's tent. Smiling she plopped down onto a rug near the cooking fire and announced, "Father has promised me to Azaz's brother."

Zipporah paused from stirring the lentil stew. "That's the young man you want, isn't it?"

"Oh yes, I've been hoping Father would accept him for me."

She hesitated and then her bright smile changed to a deep frown. "There's one problem."

"A problem? What could that be?"

Nervously, Fara twisted a strand of her hair. "Since our tribe follows the custom that the oldest daughter must take care of aging parents, you know what that means for you."

"Of course. It's tradition. My husband and I will have to live with Father."

"I'm sorry you'll have to leave your tent."

"So be it." Zipporah spoke calmly although sadness already filled her.

After the evening meal Moses entered Zipporah's part of the tent. When she saw him in the lamplight, she laid down the comb she was using to smooth her long hair. "I must tell you that Fara is promised," she told him. "After she is married, it will become my duty to care for Father."

"This is no problem," he answered amiably. "Jethro's tent is large with plenty of room for the two of us."

She bowed her head and with hands over her eyes tried to hold back the tears. Then his arms were around her and he held her to him.

"Did I say something wrong?"

"No," she sobbed. "It's my fault that we have no sons in our tent."

"Don't cry," he reassured her. "Someday the Lord will send sons to us."

Marveling at his deep faith in their God, she wiped away her tears.

At the end of Fara's betrothal year, Zipporah and Moses moved into Jethro's ample tent. Before another year had passed, Fara brought her firstborn—a daughter—for her oldest sister to hold.

Zipporah cuddled the baby against her shoulder and spoke to the child. "It seems but a short time ago that I held your mother like this."

Fara gazed wistfully at her sister. "I pray that someday you will hold one of your own."

ZIPPORAH

"Moses is sure that the Lord will send us a son, and I pray that he is right."

Each morning Zipporah's heart ached as she watched her husband walk his lonely way to care for her father's flock without sons to help him. When she carried the midmorning meal to him, she stayed longer and longer to keep him company. As the years passed, she noticed the increasing gray in his beard and hair, but he still bore himself like a prince.

Many nights she lay awake, wondering why the Lord allowed her to remain barren. Sometimes she wept, yearning to hold a baby of her own in her arms, to watch a little boy tumble around on the sheepskins and rugs, to hear his childish laughter, to see him grow up to look like his father. Other times she bowed her head in guilty relief that she would not die in childbirth and leave the child without a mother.

Lying on her bed late one night, she thought of her three sisters who were expecting babies—Misha, Jamila, and Fara. Footsteps outside the tent brought her instantly alert. No one should prowl outside at this time of night. A hand brushed the tent wall and then she heard a voice—the voice that more than twenty years before had caused her heart to flutter. Azaz!

"Come," he commanded.

Chapter 6

Zipporah sat up and whispered through the tent wall, "What do you want with me?"

"You must go to Misha." His voice took on an urgent tone. "The baby is coming too fast. You have to take care of him as soon as he's born."

"Where's Auntie? You're supposed to get her."

"She's sick and can't come."

A chill trembled through her. "Get one of her daughters. They're midwives."

"They're already there with Misha, but you're the next oldest after Auntie. It's your duty to cleanse the newborn."

Yes, it's my duty, Zipporah admitted silently as she tied on her sandals. She had watched Auntie cleanse all her newborn nieces and nephews, but had never done it herself. *When I see blood so close to me, will I faint? What if I drop the baby?* Shaking her head, she stepped out into the night.

"Hurry," Azaz ordered. "I've sent for your sisters, and now I'll wait in Achmaz' tent until someone brings news to me."

Misha's tent was astir with sisters and cousins. By the feeble light of the oil lamps Zipporah saw that Misha was already squatting over a pile of wool. She looked up at her older sister. "My tenth. You have to cleanse my tenth child." In a rush of water the baby boy emerged into the waiting hands of the oldest cousin.

As soon as the cord was cut, Zipporah held out her arms for the infant. In spite of dizziness that threatened to overwhelm her, she placed the baby on a sheepskin and began to wipe him with soft wool. Under her hands, he lay completely still. "He's not breathing!" she cried.

Misha's wail pierced the air. "Do something." Quickly Zipporah held him upside down and spanked him. Still he took no breath. Laying him on his back, she pressed his little hands against his chest, pulled them above his head and repeated the pressure. Then she placed her lips over his nose and mouth, and blew gently . . . gently. His chest expanded and he let out a healthy cry.

On her bed Misha nestled the infant while the women clustered around to offer congratulations. "The Lord has blessed you with another son." "Three daughters and seven sons—ten children altogether." Behind them, collapsed on a rug, Zipporah held her hands to her head.

A few days later Misha accosted her. "Why didn't you come sooner?"

"You mean the night your son was born?"

"Yes. Were you somewhere with my husband?"

Zipporah shook her head. "Of course not. I didn't arrive sooner because no one told me."

Misha pouted. "You've always wanted Azaz."

"That's not true. I love my husband and I want only him."

"How can you say that you love him when you refuse to give him sons?"

Shocked by her sister's question, Zipporah stumbled to her cooking fire. Later while she added oregano to the barley and lentil soup, feelings of guilt threatened to crush her. Was it fear of giving birth to a child that prevented her from holding her husband's seed?

Carrying soup in an earthen jar and flat bread in a linen cloth, she looked for Moses among the flock. With his rod on his lap, he sat leaning against a boulder. She settled herself next to him and rested while he ate.

Then he reached for her hand and they sat comfortably without speaking. Bright sunlight emphasized the gray of his beard that once had been a rich, dark brown. *He's even more handsome than when he first came to Midian*, Zipporah thought to herself.

As she admired him, she noticed a determined expression cross his face. "Someday I'll go back to Egypt." His words cut into her. He had said that before, but whenever he spoke about returning to his homeland, she always remained silent, not daring to ask when he might go or if he would take her with him to that foreign place.

The gentle mood shattered, she picked up the jar and linen cloth, and returned to her father's tent. The brisk walk helped to calm the turmoil that Moses' statement had caused.

After the next migration Zipporah struggled one morning to raise her father's heavy tent. Persistent weakness threatened to overcome her. She lay down the tent pole and crawled outside to take deep breaths of air.

Coming from her own tent, Fara knelt at Zipporah's side. "What's the matter?"

"I'm dizzy." She bowed her head and whispered, "And two moons have passed since I've had my flow."

Fara touched her sister's arm and squealed as she used to when she was a child. "It means you're expecting a baby!"

"I hope so. Do you suppose it really could be true?"

"Do you have any other signs?"

"After I eat, I don't feel well. Oh, Fara, I've waited so long—so long to have a child. Do you think the Lord has answered my prayers?"

The younger sister hugged her. "I'm sure it's true. What does your husband think about it?"

Zipporah laughed happily. "Haven't you noticed how much he's been smiling lately?"

A few moons later she could look down at a bulge under her robe. She smiled when she felt movement inside her. "Good morning, baby." At last the Lord was blessing her with a child. Before the year was finished, she would hold an infant in her arms—kiss his smooth cheek, give him milk from her breasts, warm him against her during the cold nights. All this after the child was born . . . Then she had to remind herself, "I will not be afraid of the birth. No! I will not."

Four more times the moon grew into a bright ball in the sky. One day while Zipporah ground wheat into flour, a vague cramping caused her to pause. She held her hands over the thickness of her body. Again and again the cramps persisted, but she riveted her attention on adding warm water to the flour for bread dough and then patting it into flat cakes. *I can't let the baby come*, she told herself. *What if my life blood flows away and I die?* But when a harder pain hunched her, she wiped her hands on a cloth and hurried out to find her sisters. They gathered around her. "I'll take the mid-morning meal to Moses and let him know," Tuema offered.

"And I'll tell Auntie," Duhiya said. With her arm around Zipporah, Fara led the other sisters to the tent. "The rest of us will stay with you. Our older children can take care of the younger ones."

In the tent Zipporah settled onto her bed. Auntie came

frequently to check progress, often shaking her head. "It's taking too long." As the pains increased in strength, the old midwife gave her sips of an herbal tincture.

"Why?" Zipporah cried through dry lips. "Why is it taking so long?"

Hours later she heard the sound of sheep's hooves on rocky soil . . . Moses' voice outside the tent flap . . . and then he stood by her side. She struggled to sit up, but a contraction crumpled her, bending her head toward her knees. Lovingly he touched her shoulder. "This is no place for a man. I'll wait out with the flock."

The night chill penetrated the tent walls. She heard Tarfah summon some of the sheep. A few ewes, some lambs, and one ram crowded inside.

Holding a bag of wool and a copper jug, Auntie pushed aside the tent flap and entered. Her three daughters followed with lamps, oil, and a stool. Sometime in the night Zipporah heard her aunt order, "Get these sheep out of here. We need space." Jamila and Misha called to the sheep but they refused to budge from the warmth of the tent. Fara pulled at a lamb, and with a high-pitched cry it leaped over the back of the ram. The big male jerked to his feet. As he dashed out of the tent, all the ewes and lambs followed.

Auntie set the stool on bare ground with wool arranged in front of it. "This baby will soon see the light of these lamps."

"How soon?" Zipporah cried. She had never felt such intense pain. It seized her, somewhere inside, and rose until it filled her before ebbing away. A few moments to catch her breath were all it allowed before it grabbed her again. She looked up into Fara's anxious eyes and sobbed, "Will I die?"

As if from some great distance, she heard her aunt's voice. "Fara, here's sesame oil. Rub it on her face." She felt her sister's fingers smoothing the oil across her forehead and down her cheeks, calming her fear and tenseness with the warm liquid.

Then Auntie's voice came again. "Time to put her on the stool."

Zipporah clenched her hands into tight fists. With help from Tarfah and Jamila, she was able to squat over the wool and support herself on the low stool. Her sisters and cousins formed a circle of loving concern around her. Instinctively she grasped the edges of the stool and bore down at the weight inside her.

Auntie knelt in front to catch the infant as he slipped into her waiting hands. He let out a loud cry, and she held him up for all to see. "This is a fine boy."

Zipporah's eyes blurred with tears of happiness. "Praise the Lord. I'm the mother of a son."

Auntie cut the cord with a flint knife. "Look at that fine head of hair." From the copper jug she poured camel urine onto a clean linen cloth. With it she wiped the newborn child until he shone and gave off a fragrance of pungent thyme and sweet camomile, desert herbs that the camel had eaten.

Duhiya helped Zipporah to the bed where she held out her arms for the baby wrapped now in soft woolen swaddling clothes. "How beautiful he is." She closed her eyes and cuddled him next to her breast.

A deep voice registered through her tiredness. "Peace, mother of a son." Opening her eyes she saw Moses kneeling beside the bed. "Fara came to tell me."

Smiling up at him, she pulled back the blanket to show the sleeping baby. "He looks like his father." Moses leaned down in order to see his son in the dim morning light. Lifting the baby into his arms, he spoke slowly, "Thanks to the

Lord, now there is another Hebrew in Midian, and I will name him Gershom."

"Gershom?" she questioned. "I've never heard that name before. What does it mean?"

"It means Stranger in the Land. Since I'm a sojourner and alien in Midian, so is my son." He placed the baby next to her on the bed.

"Why do you feel you're still a sojourner? You've lived here these many years and you have a covenant with my father."

"My covenant with Jethro lasts only from day to day, as long as we share food together. Since I'm a stranger here, so is my son. Gershom shall be his name when I circumcise him on the eighth day."

Instinctively Zipporah drew a blanket over the baby and held him tightly against her. Her eyes widened in horror. "Why would you want to cut a tiny baby? I see no reason to do this to a child of any age."

"It's the sign of the Lord's covenant with us." Moses spoke with determination. "Abraham circumcised his son Isaac on the eighth day, and I will do the same for my son." Without waiting for a reply, he left the tent.

No! she wanted to scream. *You mustn't cut our baby.*

Chapter 7

Desperate thoughts raced through her mind. *I'll hide with him somewhere on the eighth day. If the right time passes, maybe Moses will wait until our baby is older. But where can I hide with this little one.* She glanced wildly around. Behind the tent a ravine slashed the hillside. "I'll climb up there and find a place among the boulders," she whispered to the baby. "We'll take sheepskins and blankets to keep us warm."

She touched her cheek to her son's warm head. "No, we can't go there. Men would find us and drag us back to camp. And I can't do that to your father—shame him before the tribe and dishonor him for what he believes is right."

In her arms the baby stirred. His dark eyes opened and he nuzzled for food. She kissed his soft hair, enjoying the lingering scent of thyme and camomile. Then she held him to her breast. "I have no choice. No matter what I say, your father will circumcise you when you are eight days old."

The evening of the ceremonial day, Moses invited Achmaz and other important men of the tribe to Jethro's tent. Zipporah was ready when he came to her quarters. She stood proudly as she handed the baby to him, but as soon as he carried their son into the center room, she slumped onto a sheepskin.

Jethro stood to one side as men crowded into the center room to witness the ceremony.

Azaz entered, and with his arms folded across his chest, confronted Moses, "I will not stay to watch this barbaric action. You should wait until the boy is thirteen years old." Then he elbowed his way out of the tent.

"Stop!" Achmaz ordered. "You will stay. This is the man's tradition. He is a guest in our tribe, and we will observe the custom with him." Frowning, Azaz turned around and took a place behind the other men.

Moses removed the swaddling clothes from his son. Reluctantly Jethro held out his arms for the child. Drawing a flint knife from his belt, the baby's father passed it through the flame of the hearth fire and wiped it with a linen cloth.

Standing up to face the infant, he spoke slowly. "This is the sign of the covenant between the Lord and all the descendants of Abraham." Carefully he positioned the knife against the foreskin and cut it away. The baby let out a piercing scream.

"Your name is Gershom," Moses pronounced. He held soft woolen batting against his son's wound to stop the bleeding.

"You will offer our traditional good wishes," Achmaz ordered his men.

Grudgingly they obeyed. "May he live more than one hundred years." "May he ride well on a camel." "May he work in metal and own many sheep."

After laying down the knife and foreskin, Moses took the crying baby in his arms.

"I'll carry him to his mother now."

ZIPPORAH

"Wait!" Jethro said. "There's something more we can do."

"What more?"

The older man picked up the bloody knife and touched it to Moses' forehead and then his own. "With the blood of your son, you become a member of the Kenite tribe of Midianites."

"I do not wish to turn away from my own tribe," Moses protested. "My son and I are Hebrews, descendants of Abraham's son Isaac and of Isaac's son Jacob."

"You will always remain Hebrew. But now you and all your family have safe passage anywhere within the Kenite territory of Midian—not just from day to day but for all time. No one can change this." He looked toward Achmaz.

"So be it," the tribal leader pronounced.

"So be it," echoed the heavy voices of the tribal men.

"So be it," Moses said slowly.

In her room Zipporah had heard the baby's scream and his continued wailing. *Why didn't Moses bring him to her?* On her knees and with her head bowed to the sheepskin she waited. *Couldn't the men hurry their blood-brother ceremony? Couldn't someone bring the baby to her?*

The drape parted and Moses knelt beside her. "It's all finished. Here is our son Gershom." He placed the infant in her waiting arms. Then he held both of them close while she sobbed on his shoulder.

Not more than one moon later, Achmaz ordered the tribe to journey south toward Mount Horeb. Fara helped Zipporah roll their father's tent and load it onto a protesting camel. Its bellows echoed off the hills along with noisy cries and snorts from the other animals.

When they had everything secured for the journey,

ZIPPORAH

Hobab brought riding camels for his sisters and their children. Achmaz and Azaz led the way with goats following closely, then the sheep, pack camels, and donkeys. Tribal members rode alongside and at the end of the caravan.

Zipporah wrapped a long shawl around herself and Gershom. Riding comfortably with her feet on Tala's neck and with the baby against her breast, her thoughts turned to the awesome majesty of the mountain where the tribe was headed. In the distance she could already see its peaks.

She directed the camel closer to Fara's. "I think Mount Horeb draws us and we can't resist."

Fara held her youngest child in front of her. "And when we're there," she replied, "it watches us. If we do something wrong, it won't let us escape." She glanced suspiciously at the mountain. "When clouds hide the top, I'm afraid it will fall on us."

Zipporah's voice became hushed. "But when it's quiet and the last rays of sunlight shine on the red rocks, they turn to gold. Then the mountain is beautiful. Father says the Lord is closer to us when we are at Horeb."

"Why don't we stop talking about the mountain, and you play your flute instead?"

Zipporah reached into her saddlebag and brought out the flute. Gentle, meandering tunes might calm Fara's fears and help to diminish her own sudden uneasiness.

Three days later the tribe journeyed through a narrow pass that led to the lofty granite mountain. While the men herded the sheep and goats onto the valley floor, women unloaded camels and donkeys, raised tents, and kindled fires. Clutching waterskins, children scrambled up a deep ravine for the water that bubbled from a spring. They carried it down to troughs chiseled into low boulders by an ancestral tribe in some distant past.

After the evening meal, Moses entered Zipporah's end of the tent to hold Gershom. "Look! He's smiling at me."

She gazed fondly at her husband and son. Truly the Lord had blessed her.

As Moses handed the baby to her, he remarked, "It's always the same every time we camp at Horeb. A feeling comes over me that something strange might happen here."

"Father says that if the Lord ever wants to speak to the leader of our tribe, He will do it here."

"Why at this mountain? When the Lord spoke to Abraham it was in Canaan." A far-away look came into his eyes. "I wish I were in Egypt so I could talk to Aaron about that land the Lord promised to Abraham." He stared at the wall of the tent.

Zipporah caught her breath. *Egypt!* Confused thoughts raced through her mind. Why would Moses want to continue dwelling in a tent when he could live in Pharaoh's palace? There he could enjoy luxury and still meet secretly with his brother. Now that he had a son, an heir, couldn't he take Gershom to raise as a prince? But would he want a Midianite wife—a woman who had always slept in a tent?

She held the baby closer. Would her husband return to Egypt but leave her in Midian, lonely and disgraced in her own tribe?

Moses' voice sliced into her thoughts. "I'm waiting for the current Pharaoh to die. Then I might go to Egypt."

"Don't go." The words escaped before she could clamp a hand over her mouth.

"You don't need to worry. I won't leave yet." He hesitated before adding, "If I returned now, Pharaoh would have me executed."

"Executed!" she cried out. *What had he done?* It was not a question she dared to ask.

But bluntly the answer came. "I killed a man and tried to hide his body."

"Killed . . . killed?" she repeated, not wanting to believe what she had heard. Men killed invaders, but no one in her tribe would slay someone of their own territory. Instinctively she drew her shawl around the baby to hide him from his father's sight.

How could this man that she knew as a strong but gentle husband have murdered a man? Clutching Gershom she backed away.

Moses stepped toward her. "Let me explain."

Her body tensed and the pulse in her neck throbbed.

"One day I saw an Egyptian slave master beating a Hebrew," he told her grimly. "A Hebrew, you understand, one of my people. I couldn't endure the overseer flogging that poor man, so . . . so I struck the Egyptian with my sword and buried his body in the sand."

Imagining the bloody scene, Zipporah held her fist against her lips.

"When Pharaoh found out that I had killed one of his henchmen, he ordered my death."

Patting the baby to calm her shaking hands, she asked, "Then can you ever return to your homeland?"

"Only after Pharaoh dies."

Guilty relief spread through her. At least for now he couldn't desert her for palace life. He placed his hand on her arm. She shrank back and shifted the baby away from him. Then looking up into his face, she glimpsed his distress.

"My people are not guests of the Egyptians. They are in bondage to Pharaoh and his cruel taskmasters, but some day they will escape to the land that the Lord promised."

Hearing the anguish in her husband's voice, she no

longer cringed from his touch. He had killed to protect one of his own people. If it had been necessary, wouldn't he have done the same for her and her sisters to protect them from the invading shepherds at the well?

"No man should have to leave his own people," he said, "and become an alien in a foreign land." His arms encircled her and the baby. "From now on I will speak only Egyptian to my son."

"Egyptian?" she questioned. "Why not teach him to speak the language of his people?"

"It is nearly a lost language," he told her sadly. "Only a few, like my brother Aaron, know the tongue of our ancestors. After four hundred years in Egypt, my people speak the langauge of their oppressors. My son must learn it so he will be ready." Leaving her with the child, he went out.

She opened her robe and held Gershom to her breast, striving to use his warmth and scent to sooth the tension that ached in her heart. "Why did your father say that you must learn to speak Egyptian? Ready for what? Ready to take you to Egypt? Is that what he meant?"

Chapter 8

From that day Moses spoke only Egyptian to his son, yet he gave no further sign of returning to his homeland. Still, as seasons passed . . . and years, the nagging worry that he might take Gershom to Egypt lurked in Zipporah's thoughts.

But each day joy also swelled in her as she watched her firstborn son toddle out of the tent to play in the sunshine. He piled rocks into pillars, and laughing, knocked them over. During migration he snuggled into a saddlebag on the side of her camel.

As he grew, Zipporah yearned to have more babies, but none came. When she took the midmorning meal to her husband, Gershom walked with her. She smiled as she watched Moses lead his small son among the sheep. Then sometimes her husband would gaze at her with a sad look that said, "When will we have another son?"

While the men ate the evening meal, she sat by the side of the fire, wondering if she would become too old to produce a child. Many nights Moses came to her. Still she failed to present a secondborn to him—no new child to remind him of her love.

ZIPPORAH

As Gershom learned his father's language, Zipporah practiced it with him. While he was still small, they both became fluent in Egyptian. When the boy grew older, Moses taught him the duties of a shepherd, and from his grandfather he learned to shape flat disks of copper into bowls. Their brown-haired firstborn developed into a sturdy lad who lived the life of a shepherd during the day and a metalworker while he sat quietly with his father and grandfather in the evening.

Gershom had already celebrated his tenth birthday when the long-hoped-for signs came to Zipporah. She hummed a happy melody as she went about her work, pausing now and then to ponder about the blessing the Lord had sent and to whisper to the babe inside her, "Sleep well, little one. I love you."

Before her time, Achmaz led the tribe to the mines to trade wool for copper, then south along the turbulent waters of the sea. Finding only occasional bunches of grass for the animals, he turned the caravan north through dry river beds in the tiers of mountains. By late summer the tribe filed once more through the narrow pass that led to the foot of Mount Horeb.

As usual a feeling of reverence swept over Zipporah when the caravan approached the sacred mountain. Perhaps the tribe might camp here close to the spring of water and the ancient watering troughs long enough for her baby to see the light of day.

But the spring on the mountainside was a mere trickle and the streams in nearby valleys had gone dry. The caravan must journey on, to the west and then north, searching for grass and water.

All the next day the sun oppressed the advancing tribe. Heat waves blurred the boulders along the wadis. Near midday Zipporah felt the first cramping contractions that signaled the impending birth. "Fara," she confided to her sister riding near her, "it's beginning, but not very hard yet."

"Oh, we have a long way to travel before Achmaz will stop for the night, but I'll ride ahead to warn Auntie that the baby's coming."

"Wait, baby, wait," Zipporah implored her unborn child. "It's dangerous to stop in the heat of the day. We have to reach water before the sun sets." She sat as still as possible on Tala's hump.

When Fara returned, Auntie came too. She slowed her camel to match the pace of Zipporah's. "Tell me every time you have a pain," she said. "If they are too close, we will stop."

"Thank you, Auntie," Zipporah moaned. *Hold on, hold onto the baby*, she told herself through clenched teeth. As the caravan stretched through one narrow valley after another, the unrelenting pains tore through her body. They surged and ebbed as rhythmically as the gait of her camel. At last when the sun sank low, the welcome shouts of "Ai, ai," drifted back from the head of the caravan. Achmaz halted the tribe near a stagnant pond.

Darting to a pack camel, Fara unloaded sheepskins and made a place for her sister to lie down. Tarfah and Jamila helped Zipporah to the bed. Carrying the birthing stool and a bag of wool, Auntie rushed from her camel. "More sheepskins," she ordered. All the sisters formed a circle around Zipporah and held up the sheepskins to give some privacy. Auntie's daughters and other women gathered outside the circle to peer over the sisters' shoulders.

"Where are the husband and the brother?" Auntie shouted. "Tell them I need female camel urine right away."

The gripping pain dimmed Zipporah's awareness of the preparations for her child's birth. Then hearing Tala's loud cry, she realized that Moses or Hobab had kicked the camel's hip to make it stand up. Tala whined as someone massaged her flank until urine came.

"Duhiya, help me put your sister on the stool," the old midwife directed.

And there among the camels, the tribal women, and the circle of sisters, a new son entered the world. Auntie caught him before he could fall onto the soft wool. "It's a fine boy," she announced in a loud voice so all could hear. She cleansed the wailing infant with Tala's warm urine before she placed him in his mother's arms.

Dressed now in a clean robe, Zipporah snuggled the baby next to her on the sheepskins. The scent of pungent lavender that the camel had eaten made a pleasant fragrance on baby's skin.

Moses knelt beside them and gently laid his hand on the infant's head. Zipporah gazed lovingly at her husband. "Again the Lord has blessed us."

He looked up at the dark blue sky. "Praise the Lord for this son."

Gershom crouched next to his father. "What will you name him?"

"Eliezer."

"Is that a name of our people?"

"Yes. It means 'God is my helper.' I'll name him Eliezer because the God of my father was my help and delivered me from the sword of Pharaoh."

Gershom touched his brother's tiny fist. "I'm glad he's going to have a Hebrew name like mine."

Zipporah laid her cheek against the baby's damp hair. *So be it.* She was married to a foreigner and would abide by his choice. With effort and a catch in her voice she spoke to the sleeping child. "Eight days from now when your father circumcises you, he will name you Eliezer."

Four days later the tribe arrived at one of their territorial wells. Fara and Tuema raised their father's tent for Zipporah and she lay down to rest. Suddenly shouts rang throughout the camp. "Invaders! Invaders! They're already advancing over the next hill." The peaceful shepherds and metalworkers raced for their spears and camels. Within minutes they were warriors, ready to pursue the attackers.

Zipporah rushed out of the tent to see if Moses was riding away or if he was staying to guard the camp. From his camel he yelled to her, "If I'm not back on the eighth day, ask your father to circumcise the baby."

"Wait!" she shouted. "What if he won't do it?" But his camel was already carrying him away. Wind blew red dust into her face, and she held her hand over her nose and mouth. "What if he won't do it?" she repeated, but no one heard her.

The next morning none of the men had returned. Jethro and the other men who stayed to guard the camp had laid aside their metalworking tools to keep watch. The women waited. The day passed . . . and the next . . . and still the men failed to return.

Overcome with fear for the safety of her husband, Zipporah tossed restlessly on her bed. When visions of a bloody battle filled her mind, tears of despair wet her cheeks. "Lord," she prayed, "please bring Moses safely home to me."

On the baby's eighth morning, a fiery sun rose in the east and too soon began to descend toward the western mountains. All day Zipporah agonized over how to ask her father to perform the circumcision for Eliezer. "To do it before your thirteenth year is against our tradition," she whispered to the baby. "I don't understand why men think they must do it at all. It's such a brutal and unnecessary ceremony. But how could I explain to your father if it's not done before the sun sets today?"

Late in the afternoon she reached under the side of the tent and lifted it enough to peer at the western sky. She could no longer delay. With her son wrapped in a soft goat's wool robe, she stepped into the center room where Jethro and Gershom sat by the fire. She stood before them. "Father, I have something to ask."

"You may speak."

She took a deep breath. "My husband has not returned and it's the eighth day since the baby was born."

"What are you trying to say?"

"Will . . . you circumcise Eliezer?"

Jethro frowned at his daughter. "Why would you, a Midianite woman of the Kenite tribe, ask your father to perform this ceremony on the eighth day when that's against his belief?"

Bowing her head over the baby in her arms, she said, "My husband told me to ask you."

He shook his head. "Moses follows a strange custom. Why doesn't he wait until the child is thirteen years old? That's the proper time."

Gershom spoke gently. "My father did mine on the eighth day 'cause we're Hebrews."

"If he's not back before sundown," Jethro decided, stroking his beard, "it's a sign that the Lord doesn't want it done until the child is older. I can't go against the will of the Lord."

Holding the infant against her shoulder, Zipporah backed away and ducked into her room. With a smile of relief, she whispered to the baby, "It's the will of the Lord."

When she next looked out of the tent, only a faint orange blotch remained to light the western sky. She returned to bed and huddled with Eliezer under her blankets. At last she slept until she heard female voices shouting, "The men are coming."

In haste she pulled on an outer covering. By the moonlight illuminating the camp she could see Achmaz and Azaz dismounting. Right behind them Moses whistled for his camel to kneel. She dashed to him. "Are you all right? Are you wounded?"

He held her close and drooped his head against hers. "Only very tired, and I'm sad for those who didn't return. But I'm too weary to talk about that now."

As they walked toward the tent, he asked, "And how is our new son? Did he bleed very much?"

She stopped and clasped her hands tightly together. "My father . . . he . . . my father refused to circumcise the baby."

"Jethro refused?" The words exploded from his mouth. "How could he when he knows how important this is to me?" He let out a deep sigh. "Now our son has no covenant with the Lord."

Moses strode toward the tent and she ran to keep up with him. "He reminded me it was against his belief to do it before the child is thirteen years old."

"The eighth day has passed, but maybe I should do it anyway."

"Father said that if you didn't arrive back on time, it was the will of the Lord and you should wait until Eliezer is older."

Her husband paused a moment and considered. "The will of the Lord? Maybe you're right. I don't know. I wish I could ask Aaron's advice." For a long time he stared into the gray coals of the fire. "Will the Lord be angry with me?" he whispered once.

Outside the lamentation of the death wail rose and fell like an errant wind. The women were mourning for the men who had not returned.

Chapter 9

Finally Moses turned and held out his arms to her. "It's my fault. I should have stayed here to take care of my duty."

Slowly she walked toward him and then was in his arms. *Maybe I should admit that I don't ever want it done,* she thought, but the words would not come.

From behind the partition to his mother's room the baby whimpered and then started to cry. Reluctant to leave her husband's arms, Zipporah sighed. "I need to feed our new son."

Moses eased her away from him. "We must guard him carefully until he is circumcised and has protection from the Lord."

With tears in her eyes, she hurried to the infant. As she nursed him, Zipporah questioned if Moses was right about the covenant. Of course, like his father, her son was Hebrew. But was it true that the little child lacked the Lord's protection? Without the circumcision, would a Hebrew baby even have a name? No matter—she would call him Eliezer, the name her husband had chosen.

Raising her head, she implored, "Lord, God of Moses'

ancestors Abraham and Isaac and Jacob, protect our child."

When she first knew that Eliezer would not be cut, she had felt relief, but concern for his safety gripped her frequently during the next years. Once she dared to ask Moses if he might plan to circumcise the boy when he was thirteen.

"Don't ask me again," her husband replied. "I must wait and talk to Aaron."

Could she ever understand this man whom she loved? Sometimes he was kind and gentle—other times like distant thunder in the mountains.

In a valley near Mount Horeb a stream provided water and a comfortable camping place for the tribe. One morning Moses and his sons herded Jethro's flock west to the mountain of God.

As they left the camp, Zipporah watched proudly. Moses, still straight and regal, led the way. Gershom, now a tall young man of eighteen, followed his father. Eight-year-old Eliezer, slender and quick, had no trouble keeping up with the others. She smiled when she thought of how much both boys resembled their father—brown eyes and dark brown hair, the same color as Moses' before his turned to gray. And now Gershom's beard was beginning to grow.

Later in the day Zipporah glanced out the tent's open side. She allowed herself a few moments to gaze at the craggy top of her favorite mountain. A white cloud, etched with gray, hovered over one of the peaks. The sound of rumbling in the sky alerted her to a coming storm. Turning to the three-stoned hearth, she struck pyrite and flint until sparks ignited dry grass and tamerisk twigs.

At the sound of hooves on the rocky ground, Zipporah glanced up in surprise. She stared in amazement at her husband bringing part of the flock down from grazing. Why was he back so early? As she watched, he staggered. Dashing toward him, she called, "What's the matter?"

He lurched to her. "Let's go inside. I need to sit down."

"Where are the boys?" she asked anxiously.

"They're all right. This morning I divided the flock and sent them to another pasture." Although the afternoon was hot, Moses dropped down onto a rug by the fire. He drew a robe around his shoulders and held his hands near the flames.

She knelt next to him. "Are you sick?"

"Something strange happened to me. I saw a fire by the side of the mountain and went over to it. A flame was burning in a bush, but it didn't crumble into ashes."

Zipporah wrinkled her forehead, puzzling over what he meant. "I don't understand."

He shook his head. "Neither did I."

Not knowing what to say, she reached for his cold hands and held them between her warm ones. When he raised his head, she drew back from the wild, hunted look in his eyes.

"I heard a voice." The words stumbled from his mouth. "The Lord called to me from the bush. I answered something. I don't remember exactly what I said. Then He told me to take off my shoes because I was standing on holy ground."

The Lord! Had she understood correctly? Did he say that the God of their people had spoken to him? She leaned forward to hear more. "He told me that He is the God of my forefathers."

In her amazement she stood to her feet. "What did you do?"

His voice was low. "I hid my face because I was afraid."

If her strong husband had been frightened, maybe he really had heard a voice.

Finally he also rose to face her. "I waited while He spoke again. He told me to go back to Egypt."

"Egypt!" She stepped away from him. "Why would the Lord ask you to return there?"

"He commanded me to go. But I'm too tired to talk any more right now."

After Moses sprawled on his bed, Zipporah sat on a rug and stared absently into the fire. Egypt. Had the Lord really told her husband to go back to the land of his birth? Maybe he just imagined he had seen a burning bush that remained unconsumed and heard a voice speak to him. Or maybe it was a mirage that he had seen, shimmering heat around a yellow-flowered bush. She stared out of the tent at the rugged mountain. Of course anything could take place on the holy ground of Mount Horeb.

Hugging her knees to her chest, she rested her head on them. Would Moses really go to Egypt? Could she find the courage to ask him? Some inner alarm screamed at her, *Don't ask. You don't want to know.*

Thoughts raced through her mind. *He mustn't go back there . . . not to where Pharaoh wants to kill him.* Then she straightened up and determined, *If he returns to Egypt, I will go with him.*

The next morning she prepared a jug of camel's milk along with her husband's midmorning meal of cheese, bread, and dried dates. Following the tracks of the sheep, she came upon the flock.

Then she saw Moses. He sat against a boulder, eyes closed, both hands gripping the shepherd's rod that lay across his lap. One of her sandals slipped on a loose rock, sending the stone noisily down a small incline. He jumped to his feet. "Zipporah! You startled me!"

"I'm sorry." She offered the jug to him. "I've brought fresh milk for your midmorning meal."

ZIPPORAH

"Come sit here with me. I need to talk to you."

They sat in the shade of the boulder while she waited for him to speak. Would he tell more about the flaming bush that didn't burn?

For several minutes he studied the rod in his hands. At last he broke the silence. "Does this rod look like a serpent?" "No, it's your shepherd's rod with a knob on the end." Abruptly he announced, "I must go to Egypt."

She looked at him doubtfully. "Why?"

"The Lord has called me. The God of my forefathers, the only real God, spoke to me. I can't disregard His command."

No, you mustn't go. The unspoken words cried within her. *What can I say to convince you to stay here in the safety of the tribe?* She bit her lip and then asked, "How can you be sure it was the Lord?"

Moses shifted the rod from one hand to the other. "He gave me some signs that are impossible to ignore. I'm sure it was Him."

Riveting her attention on his shepherd's staff, she asked, "Why does He want you to return to Egypt?"

"He ordered me to talk to Pharaoh."

"No!" Her voice betrayed the alarm that threatened to turn to panic. "You told me Pharaoh wants to kill you."

Rising to his feet, Moses paced back and forth in front of her. "Wait, let me finish. Why the Lord chose me, I don't understand. My speech is slow. But I have to do this. He has commissioned me to bring the descendants of Israel out of that land."

She stumbled over her next words. "Where . . . where are you supposed to lead them?"

Her husband replied more calmly now. "To the promised land of Canaan." "Canaan! That barbaric, pagan territory?"

"It will no longer remain barbaric and pagan once the children of Israel conquer it. But first I must go to Egypt."

Slowly she drew a deep breath. "When will we leave?"

Her husband frowned at her. "I have to leave right away. You will stay here with your father."

His words were the ones she had always dreaded she might hear. For a moment she closed her eyes to shut them out. *He's grown tired of me. Moses doesn't want me any longer. He'll take our sons to Egypt and will find a new wife from his own tribe.* Trying to keep her voice from shaking, she pleaded, "I want to go with you."

Sadly he reached down and pulled her up into his arms. "It's a dangerous journey. Have you ever been out of your tribal territory?"

"No," she admitted.

"Amalekite tribes roam through the wilderness. They attack any caravan, large or small, that they choose. I don't want anything to happen to our sons and to you."

Our sons! He had not planned to take them away. Moses was only concerned over the safety of his family. With her heart full of love, she raised her face to his. "I still want to go wherever you go."

"And in Egypt," he continued, "only the Lord knows what will happen there."

Now her voice assumed a note of determination. "Midianites are not afraid of Egyptians."

His firmness matched hers. "You don't know Egyptians as well as I do."

"We will have you to protect us. I'll never forget what you did for my sisters and me long ago at the well."

"All right," he agreed reluctantly, "you can start out with me, but if we run into any risk, for your safety I'll have to send you and the boys back."

ZIPPORAH

As she returned to the camp, she had time to enjoy the satisfaction of success. Her husband would not go away and forget her. But she hoped they would hurry back to Midian, to the mountains and valleys, to the security of the family and the tribe.

After Zipporah served the evening meal to her family, she went to her quarters to concentrate on packing. Later Moses lifted the partition. The dim light of the oil lamps revealed a collection of saddlebags and clothing. Seated by a pile of bowls, she glanced up at her husband. "Tala's too old to make such a long journey. I'll choose a good milking female to ride. Of course we'll have to take her calf along. Then we'll need at least one pack animal in addition to the riding camels for you and the boys."

"We're not taking any camels."

"None!" she exclaimed. "It's impossible for a family to travel without them."

He rubbed his forehead with one hand.

"I think it would be better if you and our sons stayed here."

She folded her hands into tight fists. "Why can't we take camels?"

"There are only a few in Egypt. If we arrive on these big animals, soldiers will detain us for questioning. They even search merchant caravans. We'll take a donkey for you and Eliezer to ride on."

"Donkeys are pack animals. People ride on camels."

"In Egypt people ride on donkeys," he replied. "We'll take one."

"Only one? I have to pack food and sheepskins and . . .

"You're right. Take one more but that's enough."

"Without camels for protection against wind and sand," she fretted, "how will we sleep?"

"In the shelter of rocks and there are a few lodging places along the way." He turned and went out.

His words echoed in her mind. *The lodging places—will they have walls around them? I've never slept behind a wall. How will we escape if invaders attack?*

Chapter 10

But now she must dismiss the distressing thought and concentrate on packing. Into two saddlebags she placed food, cooking equipment, flint, and pyrite. For drawing water she chose a leather bucket and goatskin pouches to store it as they traveled.

"Metal," she murmured, "I will need some metal for trading." Carefully she unfolded a shawl and removed her wedding veil from it. For a moment she held the soft cloth, and smiled as she remembered her wedding day . . . the long wait in Auntie's tent . . . the festively decorated camel that Hobab brought for her to ride . . . Moses as he stood in front of her.

Setting her mouth into a determined line, she took a knife and cut away all the copper and silver disks from the veil. More possessions lay in front of her. On an impulse she selected her flute and the curved throwstick.

After the evening meal Zipporah lay down wearily on her sheepskins. During the night she awakened suddenly. What was it? The tent vibrated although no wind blew.

Hearing Moses' footsteps in the center room, she left her bed and lifted the partition. In the bright moonlight her husband stood by the tent's open side. She touched his arm. "What has happened?"

"Just now the Lord spoke to me again."

Stunned, she held onto his arm.

"He said that all the men in Egypt who were seeking my life are dead."

She sighed in relief. "Then you are out of danger."

He took both of her hands in his and held them while he gazed at her upturned face. "All I know is what the Lord told me." Then he let out a deep groan. "Why has He chosen me for this great task? How can a man who speaks so slowly become a leader?"

"The Lord promised to help. You told me that He gave some signs to use."

Letting go of her hands, Moses stood for a moment in deep thought before he said, "Two days from now we need to leave for Egypt."

"That soon?"

"Yes," he replied before staggering back to the room where Jethro, Gershom, and Eliezer were sleeping. When the partition hid him from Zipporah's sight, a new worry thrust itself into her mind. *What sort of man was the present ruler of Egypt?*

The next morning she walked slowly to Fara's tent. The youngest sister knelt in the center, grinding wheat in a granite mortar.

Even after having eight children, she still looks young, Zipporah mused.

Fara rose to her feet. "When do you leave for Egypt?"

"Tomorrow."

"So soon!"

Zipporah nodded. "Will you come with me to say goodbye to the others?"

ZIPPORAH

"Of course."

With arms around each other, they went from tent to tent—Tuema's . . . Duhiya's . . . Tarfah's . . . Jamila's. And then Zipporah said, "I think I should go alone to Misha."

"Perhaps that is better."

Now that Azaz was second in command of the tribe, his tent was larger than any of the others except for that of Achmaz. Misha sat by her fire, fingering the newest silver necklace that Azaz had fashioned for her. She already wore necklaces of turquoise and gold. Silver bracelets jingled on her wrists.

"May this sister enter your tent?" Zipporah asked.

"Enter."

"I leave tomorrow for Egypt."

Misha frowned. "Why are you deserting your tribe? Have you no loyalty?"

"I'm loyal to my husband. I will go with him to his homeland."

"And leave me with your responsibilities."

"You've always wanted to be the oldest daughter."

Misha stood up and her dark eyes flashed. "As soon as you're gone, it's my duty to take care of Father. Azaz and I will have to leave our comfortable tent and move into his."

"I'm sorry."

The younger sister stared into the fire. "And . . . and will I ever see you again?"

"I hope so." Zipporah touched her hand. "Remember how we used to signal to each other with our flutes?"

Her sister swallowed hard. "And we always protected each other and the little girls."

They stood together in silence until Misha withdrew her hand. "But, now you are deserting me."

Zipporah hurried out of the tent to search for Hobab

among the camels. She found him brushing Tala.

"You are doing right," her brother reassured her. "It's a woman's duty to follow her husband."

"First I must say goodbye to Tala." Hobab left her alone with her pet. Zipporah laid her head against the old camel's warm side. Tears came. *Will I ever see any of my sisters or my brother or my father again? How can I live away from the safety of the tribe?*

Tala nuzzled and searched at Zipporah's waistband for dates.

"I haven't forgotten your treat," she said as she allowed the animal to nibble the dates from her hand.

As the next morning's sun struck the red granite mountains, Zipporah tied their supplies onto the pack donkey. Shivering in the cold, Eliezer jumped up and down to keep warm. As she tightened the last knot, she noticed her father walking from his tent.

He stopped in front of her and held out a small leather bag. "I have guarded your bride-price until you would need it. Now I want you to take it with you."

She stared at the bag in his hand. Although the gold was rightfully hers, she hesitated. To accept it from her father's safekeeping would cut her apart from the family security she had always known. Slowly she reached for it, and then to hide the tears in her eyes, she busied herself with packing the gold into a saddlebag.

Behind her, Moses' voice rose in the still morning air. "Jethro, I wish you were going with me. I could use your advice and guidance in this mission that the Lord has called me to do."

"The Lord has spoken to you," his father-in-law replied, "but He has not called me to lead the Israelites out of Egypt." He handed a goatskin pouch to Moses. "Take this

set of metalworking tools with you. Some day you might
need them."

Then he went to his grandsons and kissed them. After
kissing his daughter and his son-in-law, he pronounced his
blessing, "Go now in peace." With head bent, he turned
toward his tent. As he walked away, Zipporah heard him
mutter, "The Lord has spoken. A mere man must not object
when part of his family leaves him."

Gershom brought the riding donkey. Moses ran his hand
over its back. "I chose the best one I could find for you to
ride," he said to Zipporah.

"Eliezer can ride," she replied as she placed sheepskins
on the donkey's back. "I will walk."

"Not while we leave the camp. I want to show these
proud Midianites that my wife will ride."

"I too am Midianite," she mentioned softly.

"You are married to me. Why can't you think of yourself
as Hebrew?"

"Because I am not."

"I'll help you get on the donkey."

"Do I get to ride too?" Eliezer shouted.

"Yes, son." He lifted the boy to a place behind his
mother. Then Moses surveyed his little caravan. "I will lead
the way. Gershom, you will follow me with the pack animal,
and then your mother and Eliezer on the riding donkey."
Looking straight ahead, he strode toward the pass that led
away from the mountain of God.

As they passed Achmaz' tent, the tribal chieftain and
Azaz silently watched.

Hobab stood in front of his tent. "Go with God," he said
as they passed.

"Stay with God," they replied.

In the dim morning light Zipporah's sisters were a

sobbing cluster of dark-robed figures.

And then the camp was behind her. Zipporah glanced back once. The black tents spread across one side of the valley. Above them Mount Horeb's peaks were lost in gray clouds.

Sadness filled her. She was leaving the sacred mountain behind her. Would she ever see it again? Even worse, she was abandoning her family and her homeland, going off without a tent, with no camel to crouch behind during a sandstorm, no loom for weaving cloth. But it was a journey that she had chosen. She had insisted that her husband take her with him to the land of the Nile River. Her sadness was of her own making. If he had left without her, much greater heartache would now weigh her down.

Did he realize that it was out of love for him that she was parting from her land and her family?

As soon as the tents disappeared from sight, she slipped off the donkey and plodded alongside. Unaccustomed to traveling on foot, Zipporah soon felt the discomfort of stones under her sandals. *How foolish to go off without camels!* Before long the sun beat down on the small group as they threaded their way through a narrow wadi.

"We'll head north to the high cliffs and then turn west," Moses announced to Gershom.

The high cliffs! She had seen them from a distance but had never been near. That land was beyond her territory, beyond the design of mallets chiseled onto the side of boulders to mark the tribal boundaries. Only unknown regions lay ahead.

Four days later the great cliffs rose in front of the travelers. They stopped to rest under a thorny acacia tree.

"This is where we turn west along the caravan route to

the sea," Moses explained. "Tonight we'll sleep in one of the caves along the cliffs."

A *cave*, Zipporah thought, remembering the safety of her tent and the comfort of sleeping next to a camel under the stars. *I'll feel enclosed in a cave.* Too weary to object, she rested with Eliezer stretched out on the ground beside her. The sweet fragrance of acacia blossoms hovered in the hot air.

Accustomed to years of constant alertness, she was the first to detect the approach of strangers. "Camels coming," she warned. "I can hear leather saddlebags rubbing." Before the family could hide, a caravan appeared around a bend in the trail. Ishmaelites.

Moses approached their leader. "Peace."

"Peace," replied the Ishmaelite as he halted the column.

"Is it safe to travel this route to the sea?" Moses inquired.

"I advise against it. We set out from near here yesterday but turned around when we heard that an Amalekite tribe was raiding caravans. Since we're loaded with trade goods for Egypt, we considered it wise to retreat."

"Which way will you travel?"

The Ishmaelite pointed to the cliffs. "There's a hidden pass that leads to the plateau. Then we'll go north to the mountain of God before we turn west."

"The mountain of God?"

The leader laughed. "You appear to be a Midianite so of course you think Horeb is the only holy mountain. I assure you there's another one to the north. It's our landmark." He glanced toward the acacia tree where Zipporah and the boys waited. "You're welcome to journey with us. Where are your camels?"

Moses shook his head. "We have no camels, only donkeys."

"No camels! Then we can't wait for you." He raised his hand, and the caravan turned onto a trail that led to the hidden pass.

Zipporah left the shade of the tree. "I heard what he said."

"I'll take his advice. We'll travel north instead of west." Moses returned to the donkeys. "But it's late today." He pointed toward the cliffs. "I see a cave where we can camp."

They hid the animals near the back of the cave behind a pool of stagnant water. During the night Zipporah woke up often, coughing from the cave's musty air and shivering from thoughts of Amalekites. Amalekites, the fiercest and most warlike of tribes.

Before dawn Moses led the way up the pass. At the top of the steep trail, Zipporah paused to look back. The first rays of morning sun struck the southern mountains, highlighting their savage splendor. In the distance one rose in solitary majesty—Mount Horeb. She turned to face north. A bleak plain—white sand sprinkled sparsely with dry, red pebbles—stretched ahead.

Day after day they traveled north. Sometimes Zipporah rode the donkey. Other times she trudged on foot behind Moses and their sons. For protection against blowing sand and burning sun, she pulled a shawl across her face. At night she huddled with Eliezer, warming him from the harsh cold. A few white clay hills held caves. In them, the water remaining from rain months before resembled the color of sheep's milk.

One day Moses stumbled to a stop. "I think I see a lodging place ahead of us."

"Praise to the Lord, the God of our forefathers," his wife sighed. "Even an inn is better than this endless white desert."

"I hope it's not a mirage," Moses added wearily. They came to a limestone wall that surrounded a two-story building, a large courtyard for animals, and a smaller area for cooking fires. After Zipporah untied the packs, Gershom and Eliezer helped her carry saddlebags and sheepskins up narrow stairs to a small room.

Stopping at the doorway, she drew in a sharp breath. Moses lay sprawled, face down, on the floor.

Chapter 11

Quickly she spread out a sheepskin and with Gershom's help rolled him onto the wool. "What is it? What's the matter?" With his hand over his eyes he replied, "I don't know."

"Are you in pain?"

He didn't answer.

"Stay here with your father," she told her sons. "I need to get some water." Grabbing the leather bucket, she raced down the stairs and into the courtyard to draw water from a well.

When she returned to the room, Zipporah knelt by her husband's side. Was he breathing? She laid her head against his chest and detected a faint heart beat. His lips moved and barely audible words came. "I have sinned. The Lord is angry with me. I failed . . . I failed to circumcise my second son." Then he appeared to stop breathing.

"Don't die," she implored. "Oh, don't die." Searching for help, she glanced around the small room but saw only the saddlebags, the bucket of water, and her two sons immobilized in mute shock.

She wet a cloth and laid it across Moses' forehead.

"It's my fault," she whispered to him. "Mine . . . because I didn't want it done."

His reply was a low moan. He reached for her hand and struggled to get up. "I have to circumcise Eliezer." Too weak to sit, he sank back onto the sheepskin with one arm across his forehead. "I have to circumcise . . ." he repeated before the words died in his throat.

In horror, Zipporah screamed, "No, don't die." Turning to Gershom, she ordered, "Take my knife down to some woman's cooking fire and pass it through the flame. Hurry!"

He dashed away with the knife. Eliezer stood in front of his mother.

"Son," she said as calmly as she could, "you know your father and your brother are both circumcised. Now it's your turn."

The boy's eyes widened. "No! That'll hurt."

"Yes, but you must be brave."

"I'm not old enough," he protested. "I'm supposed to be thirteen."

Zipporah glanced at Moses. "Your father is Hebrew. That makes you Hebrew, too, so we can't wait until you're thirteen."

Gershom hurried into the room with the flint knife. "Mother, are we going to circumcise Eliezer?"

"I'll do it."

"How can you when you can't stand the sight of blood? Let me do it?"

She bit her lip. "That wouldn't be right. It's my responsibility. I'll have to do it."

"Nobody's going to touch me," Eliezer shouted, holding his robe tighter around his legs. "I'm not going to show myself in front of you."

Moses tried to sit up. "I must circumcise my son. I must

. . ." With a loud groan, he fell backward. Gershom grabbed his brother and wrestled him to the floor. He pinned the boy's arms to his sides. Unable to move his arms, Eliezer kicked wildly.

Taking a clean cloth, Zipporah wiped the knife. "Don't cut me," Eliezer screamed. "It'll hurt."

She sat down on his bare feet. "Now, hold still or I might cut too far."

He rolled his head from side to side. "No! No!" When Gershom lay on top of him, Eliezer stopped struggling.

His mother positioned the knife, but hesitated. Her throat was closing, shutting off the air. She tried to swallow but found it impossible. The knife became a blur in her hand. I *mustn't faint. I mustn't.* She shook her head and the blur cleared. With her lips pressed in a firm line, she carefully made an incision.

The boy's screams filled the room and he wildly fought against his mother and brother.

"I'm almost finished." She removed the skin and placed soft wool on the wound before pronouncing, "Your name is Eliezer."

He continued to scream while Gershom held more wool to the wound to stop the bleeding.

Zipporah stared at the blood on her hand and then fell onto the sheepskin next to her husband. When conscious-ness returned, Eliezer's screams had turned into deep sobs. Moses gave no sign of movement. She looked at the severed skin, still clutched in her hand. "I should put blood on your forehead," she said.

But one of his arms lay across his face. A robe covered the rest of his body except for his feet. She touched them · with the foreskin and said softly, "Surely now you are a bridegroom of blood to me."

"Mother, what are you doing?" Gershom asked.

"I'm making a covenant with your father. On our wedding night I refused to accept his tribe as mine." She placed her lips close to Moses' ear. "Forgive me, I was wrong. With this blood I receive the covenant that you offered long ago."

Had he heard? Did he understand?

Suddenly he opened his eyes. "What happened? Did I hear Eliezer screaming?" He raised himself on one elbow.

"Yes, because I circumcised him." Her voice shook. "And with his blood on you and me, I accept the covenant you offered on our wedding night. You are a bridegroom of blood to me."

Moses held out his arms to her, and she collapsed onto his broad chest. Smiling up at his two sons, he said, "I did not take my people's covenant with the Lord as seriously as I should have. But He has released me from my guilt and let me come back to my family." His voice became stronger with each word. "We'll stay here for a few days until Eliezer is well enough to ride on a donkey. Now we must eat and then rest."

Trembling and exhausted, Zipporah agreed, "Yes, we must eat and rest." She searched in a saddlebag until she found her copper bowl. Descending the stairs she stopped to lean her head against the wall. When the cold stones sent a chill through her, she strugged on.

A cooking fire in the smaller courtyard gave a welcome glow. The woman squatting by the fire glanced up.

"Do you have camel's milk?" Zipporah asked. The woman nodded.

Reaching into the fold of her waistband, Zipporah brought out a copper disk. "Will you trade milk for this?"

"You look very tired," the woman answered. "I'll be glad

to give milk for the copper." She pointed to the fire. "And you may prepare your meal here." In the way of the desert she did not ask Zipporah what had happened in the upper room to cause Eliezer to scream.

Zipporah bowed her head. "I am grateful." As soon as the milk was hot, she carried it up the stairs and added crushed cardamom seeds. "Here is a soothing drink for you," she offered to her husband. He drank from the bowl and then handed it to Eliezer. After both her sons had drunk, she too relaxed with the aromatic milk. Later when she brought boiled wheat for supper, her younger son already slept.

During the next days she watched Eliezer carefully for any sign of bleeding. As soon as the boy's wound healed, Moses led his family north across the flat wilderness.

Now a great mountain, the Ishmaelites' landmark, loomed out of the desert plain and drew them on. During the days it appeared like a shimmering mirage and in the evenings lavender and blue shadows softened its rugged shape.

Gershom was the first to sight palm trees at the mountain's base. "An oasis," he shouted. The family pushed ahead to the lonely camping place. The palm trees surrounded a spring of clear water, a welcome change from the hot desert sand.

Moses stood in the shade of a tree and declared, "The Lord has prepared this good resting place for us."

While Gershom and Eliezer led the donkeys to drink, Zipporah struck sparks for a fire. As soon as a nest of dry grass ignited, she added dry camel dung she found around the campsite.

After pouring water into a palm-frond bowl, she put in a bit of salt and ground wheat. Then she formed flat loaves from the dough and baked them in the fire's hot ashes.

A juglet from her pack held a small amount of clarified butter, liquid and still sweet. She rolled dates in the butter and inserted them into the hot bread. *The meal satisfies hunger*, Zipporah reflected while her husband and sons ate, *but it would taste better if we had a camel to provide fresh milk.*

A solitary traveler at the edge of the camp caught her eye. He carried a small pack, and with weary steps plodded toward the spring.

Before she could speak, Eliezer's hushed voice announced, "I see a man."

His father turned to look. "Come with me, Gershom. We will find out who this stranger is." With a determined stride he led the way.

Zipporah watched while the men talked. Then they embraced and kissed each other.

Gershom ran toward the fire. "It's Uncle Aaron."

His mother laid down the bread she was eating. "Your father's brother?"

"How did he find us all the way out here?" Eliezer asked.

"Father said that the Lord directed him."

Zipporah arose to her feet. "It's our duty to welcome your father's brother."

"I'll lead the way," Gershom said.

"That's proper," she agreed. "Eliezer and I will follow."

They stopped a few feet to the side of Moses and waited respectfully.

Aaron's gaze examined Zipporah. "So this is the woman who is your wife."

Moses glanced proudly at her. "My wife Zipporah."

"She doesn't look like a Hebrew."

"She was born the daughter of Jethro, priest of the Kenite tribe of Midian, but through my covenant with her, she is Hebrew of the tribe of Levi." He laid his hand on his brother's shoulder. "Come now to our camp and accept our hospitality."

Zipporah spread a sheepskin by the fire for Aaron to sit on. Then she removed his sandals and poured water over his feet and his hands. After baking the last of the bread dough, she prepared it with butter and dates for her brother-in-law's evening meal.

Later with Eliezer asleep beside her, she listened to her husband and Aaron talking. Gershom sat silently near them.

Aaron's voice took on a harsh note. "With the new ruler, oppression is worse than ever. The time has come for our people to rebel."

"The Lord told me," Moses replied.

"The Lord spoke to me also and showed me that I must meet you here because He has chosen you to go to Pharaoh and then lead our people out of Egypt."

Moses sighed deeply. "Yes, He has commissioned me. But why me?" He stood and stared into the starlit sky. "Someday He will come to lead His people. Why doesn't He come now?"

"Someday," Aaron repeated, "but this time He has called you. If you tell me what to say, I'll speak for you."

The next morning the two brothers led the way westward along the well-used caravan route into a wide valley. A sparse scattering of prickly bushes grew on the valley floor. By evening they made camp in the protection of a low hill.

As Zipporah drifted to sleep, Aaron's voice brought her suddenly alert.

"Moses," he said, "Egypt is no place for this Midianite woman."

"This woman is my wife."

"You should have relayed a message to me," the brother insisted. "Miriam and I know ways to smuggle someone out of the country. We could have sent a Hebrew woman to you."

"I am content with the daughter of Jethro," Moses said firmly, "and I've already told you that I have a covenant with her."

"Even so, Egypt is no place for her. Pharaoh will object to letting our people leave. The result will be danger and suffering for everyone, including this woman and your sons."

With concern in his voice Moses replied, "Of course I want safety for her and my sons."

"Then why is she here?"

"She begged to come."

"And you allowed her?"

"I did, and now what can I do?"

Aaron's voice was emphatic. "You can send her and your sons back to your father-in-law."

"I can't let them travel alone across the desert."

"You'll have to find a way to do it."

Zipporah held tight fists over her eyes to blot out her fear. *Will he really send us back?* For a long time she lay awake. A half moon rose and drifted slowly across the sky while frightening thoughts circled in her mind. *With Moses I feel safe, but without him . . .*

In the distance a desert predator howled.

Two days later Moses shouted back over his shoulder, "I can see water and the trees of a large oasis."

Zipporah jabbed her heel onto the side of the donkey and hurried it forward. Yes, there was the oasis, thanks to the Lord, and what looked like an encampment of Ishmaelites.

At the oasis she slid off the donkey and tied on her sandals. In the welcome shade of tamerisks, she unpacked barley and firelighting stones. Soon bright flames flickered across her fire. She picked up the water pouch and started to walk to the large spring but stopped in surprise.

Moses and an Ishmaelite faced each other as if they were making an agreement. Then Moses reached into the folds of his wide woolen waistband and handed something to the other man.

After filling the pouch with water, Zipporah returned to the fire. Her husband stood there, staring into the flame. "I had some gold that I've saved all these years since I left Egypt."

"And you gave it to the Ishmaelite?"

He turned to face her. "Most of it. These traders are proceeding down the caravan route by the Red Sea and then east to Midian. I . . . I have arranged for you and Gershom and Eliezer to travel with them."

Chapter 12

A t first she was speechless. Finally she managed to stammer, "Without you? How can I go without you?"
He took her hands in his. "After Aaron and I arrive in Egypt, suffering will come to both the Hebrews and Egyptians. I want to spare you from seeing all that, and I want to protect you and our sons from danger."

Tears ran down her cheeks. "There will be danger for you too."

"The Lord has told me to go, and I must."

She wiped her wet face on the sleeve of her robe. "When will I ever see you again?"

"I'll return as soon as possible." He touched his forehead to hers. "Take sheepskins and whatever you need from the donkey's packs. The Ishmaelites have camels for you to ride and plenty of food. Their leader has promised to take you home."

"Home." The word was a sob in her throat. "Yes, our sons will be safe there."

At dawn the next morning Moses walked with his family to the nomads' camp. As she followed her husband, Zipporah reflected on the many times she had worried about a separation from him. Now it was happening.

The leader waited by the side of his camel. "I have two fine riding camels for your sons and your wife." He led the way to the animals—already saddled for the day's journey.

Zipporah drew in a sharp breath. A large, evil-appearing male camel glared at her. Then she breathed a sigh of relief. The other was a young female with a long-legged calf.

Moses put down the sheepskins he carried and took Zipporah into his arms. "May the Lord protect you." He kissed her and silently she clung to him while Gershom and Eliezer waited for their turns to say goodbye to their father. After kissing them, he gave his blessing, "Go with God."

She watched him walk away. "Lord, protect him from Pharaoh," she prayed, "and from all danger . . ."

Eliezer's voice broke into her prayer. "I want to go with Father."

"You can't," Gershom grumbled. "You're too little, and anyway, last night I asked if I could and he said 'no.' If I can't, he's not going to take you."

"Don't tell me what I can't do," the little boy shouted.

"Quit yelling," his older brother ordered. "You're not going to Egypt."

"Why not?"

"Eliezer and Gershom," Zipporah snapped, "stop arguing."

"Mother," Gershom announced, "Father told me to take his place as head of the family while he's gone. I can make decisions." He stood in front of her. "You must hurry and pack the sheepskins and saddlebags onto the camels. The caravan is ready to leave."

"Yes, son, you are right."

"Eliezer and I will ride the male," he informed her. "The female is for you."

ZIPPORAH

With satisfaction she noted the authority in his voice. *My firstborn. Not long ago this tall young man was a boy like Eliezer. Now he's carrying out the responsibility his father assigned to him.*

Padding the camel saddles with sheepskins and securing the saddlebags, she did not notice the approach of the Ishmaelite leader. He stood behind her. "So your husband grew tired of you and is sending you away."

She looked at him in shock. How could he insult her after he had accepted her husband's gold?

"Not true." Gershom placed himself between his mother and the Ishmaelite. "My father is sending her back to Midian for her own safety."

The leader muttered something that sounded like a growl and walked away.

Zipporah smiled at her son. She and Moses had raised a strong young prince.

The caravan headed south. Before nightfall they camped by the sea, among wind-tossed sand dunes and seashells. One of the Ishmaelite women approached Zipporah with barley, raisins, and buttermilk. "Our leader said I should take food to you. You may prepare it for your sons and yourself at my fire."

"You are very kind."

The woman's face softened. "It's not easy to travel without a husband. I know. Mine was killed many years ago when Amalekites raided our camp."

"How sad for you."

Suddenly the guards at the edge of the camp shouted, "Camels are coming from the south."

"Danger!" The woman grabbed Zipporah by the arm and together they hurried to where everyone clustered near the leader. "Another Ishmaelite tribe is approaching," he said, "but we can see that there are only a few of them." He waited until the lead camel halted in front of him.

ZIPPORAH

A man with a bloody gash on his face was the first to speak. "Amalekites. Without warning they attacked and robbed us. You know the place by the sea where hills can hide their warriors?"

"I know the place."

"You must turn back, and we beg permission to travel with you."

"You have it," the leader answered and then he shouted to the people, "Mount your camels. This night we'll head north. Our caravan now goes to Canaan and Damascus instead of to Midian."

Canaan and Damascus! The words struck fear into Zipporah. *When would we ever reach home if this caravan goes as far as Damascus?*

But even more frightening was the thought of meeting Amalekite warriors. Along with her sons she raced for the camels and flung sheepskins and saddles on the animals' backs. Grabbing the saddlebags, she mounted and whistled for her camel to stand up.

The two tribes made a quick departure from the camping place. They traveled through the night, and the next day turned toward the mountain where Aaron had come to meet Moses. *Where is my husband now?* Zipporah ached to know. *Have he and his brother safely passed the Egyptian border guards? Lord, watch over them.*

Soon we'll arrive at that northern mountain. To the east the route leads to Canaan and then to Damascus. No! I don't want to go there. Could we go to Midian instead? She gazed south and thought of the vast desert they had crossed when Moses led them north. Without him could she and Gershom and Eliezer survive a trip through the barren wilderness? What would they need for the journey?

When the tribes camped at the mountain, Zipporah

approached the leader. "May this woman ask a question?"

"You may ask."

"I wish to have the two camels that my sons and I are riding."

The leader gave a disgusted laugh. "Your husband paid me only enough for you to use the camels, not own them."

"I have gold."

His face showed no reaction. "How much?"

"How much do you want for the two camels?"

"These are strong, young camels worth much gold."

She hesitated before offering, "One *deben* of gold for each camel."

The Ishmaelite held his hand over his eyes. "The gods forbid that I should let two fine camels go for such a pittance. They are worth at least ten times that much.

No, they are not, she thought, *and fifteen debens is all I have.* "For both camels I will pay four *debens.*"

The man spat on the ground. "I will accept nothing less than eight."

Zipporah started to walk away.

"Six," he called to her, "but the female's calf stays with me."

"Six for the two camels with their saddles."

"So be it," he said.

"So be it. I will bring the gold so you can weigh it." She turned away to hide her smile. Six—the amount she had decided on before she started to bargain.

After she handed over the gold, Zipporah carried a saddlebag to another Ishmaelite to bargain for grain, dates, raisins, and an extra water pouch. He accepted some of the copper and silver disks that she had cut from her wedding veil.

She loaded the supplies into the bag, and as she

struggled to lift it, Gershom stood by her side. "Why are you buying food? Father already paid."

"We're going home."

"We can't go all that way without the donkeys that Father took with him."

"I have bought camels."

He frowned. "You have made these decisions without asking me?"

She set down the bag and faced the tall young man who was her son. "It is my privilege to use my bride-price and the disks from my wedding veil as I wish," she said softly. "Eliezer and I are not going to Damascus. We're going home. Will you come with us?"

"Father instructed me to take care of you and Eliezer. He even left some of his gold for me." Gershom picked up the heavy bag and slung it over his shoulder. "Let's go."

The next morning even before the Ishmaelites left camp, Zipporah loaded the small amount of equipment and supplies onto the camels. The woman who had befriended her approached with a gourd in her hand. "I have brought clarified butter for you."

For a moment Zipporah couldn't speak. While on migration, it was not easy to make butter and then boil it and skim away the solids to prevent it from becoming rancid. "I am grateful for your kindness," she finally managed to say.

"Go with God," the woman said.

"Stay with God," Zipporah replied, and then she and her sons rode away from the mountain. A yearning for home washed over her, followed quickly by a lurking concern. *How will the tribe receive us when we arrive without Moses?*

A range of mountains rose as a barrier to the west. By evening when the sun had vanished behind it, they halted their two camels at a camping place. A twisting trail led into a ravine where the low growth of lacy tamarisks indicated water. Taking the empty water pouches, Zipporah walked to the spring. After the hot journey during the day, this lonely place provided a welcome rest. Delicate maidenhair fern ringed the small pool. Nearby a bulbul sang its soft and plaintive song.

Zipporah filled the pouches and then closed her eyes, allowing her fatigue to drain away. *What is my husband doing now?* she wondered. *Has he already gone before Pharaoh and demanded release of the people? Maybe Pharaoh put him in prison . . . or worse . . . no, the Lord commissioned him to lead the Israelites. The Lord is with him.*

And if he brings them safely out, will he return to Mount Horeb for more messages from the Lord? She shook her head. *Achmaz is a stern man and would never allow all those Hebrew tribes in his territory.*

Suddenly her body tensed. A slight breeze brought the wild, musty odor of desert cat. Cautiously she opened her eyes. From a bend in the trail, a leopard stared at her.

Chapter 13

The leopard stood motionless, one wide forepaw ahead of the other. A low ray of sunshine brushed the large cat's tawny fur and emphasized its black spots.

Instinct, coupled with early training, warned Zipporah to remain completely still. *I'm in his territory, but if I try to leave, he might attack. And my throwstick is back at the camp.*

Watching steadily, the leopard stepped off the trail. His body rippled in silent grace to the base of a tamarisk. There he crouched, his long tail twitching.

Zipporah hardly dared to breath. *I must let him know that I'm only passing through his territory. But how?* Without further thought she said gently, "Peace."

The leopard raised his head and his tail became motionless. Then he stood, and with one last, haughty glance in her direction, disappeared behind the tamarisk trees.

She picked up her water pouches and walked cautiously out of the ravine. "Leopard," she breathed out the word to Gershom and Eliezer. "Don't make any quick movements. Just help me load the camels. We must leave this cat's territory."

Eliezer stood like a rock until Gershom tapped him on

the shoulder. "Come on, we have to help Mother." Glancing frequently toward the ravine, they replaced the saddles and sheepskins, saddlebags and pouches onto the animals. The male snorted nervously and the female whined.

After mounting and leaving the camp, they continued cautiously until well past the ravine. They traveled far into the night before stopping by the side of the trail. Zipporah took time only to milk the camel and give raisins and milk to her sons before she slept.

Early the next day they continued across the vast plateau, following dry wadis. The camels halted occasionally and with their long, thin lips plucked the spiny bushes.

There was a sameness about each day until one morning Zipporah's camel refused to stand up.

"What's the matter with it?" Eliezer asked.

His mother shook her head. "I don't know."

"I remember once when Grandfather's riding camel wouldn't get up," Gershom said. "He poured liquid butter into its nose and it got well."

Eliezer frowned. "How did butter make it get well?"

"Maybe it just made the camel so mad that it didn't want to stay sick any longer, or maybe it wasn't sick at all, just stubborn."

Zipporah shook the gourd that held the clarified butter. "There's still some in here."

"I'll get some sticks so Eliezer and I can keep the camel from biting you."

With the gourd ready, she stood in front of the animal. Gershom and Eliezer poked at its neck with their sticks. The camel raised its head and showed big, yellow teeth. Quickly Zipporah poured the butter into its nose.

The camel coughed and sneezed before letting out a raucous cry. Then it rocked to its feet and spat at her. She jumped away with a satisfied laugh. "Thanks to the Lord and the Ishmaelite woman who gave me this butter, we no longer have an unwilling camel."

"Let's saddle up and get going," her older son replied.

Near evening Gershom and Eliezer rode ahead to the top of a slight rise. "I see the lodging where we stayed when we traveled north with Father," Eliezer called to his mother.

For a moment she shuddered with the memory of Moses' illness and Eliezer's circumcision. Then remembering the covenant with her husband, she sighed happily.

"Are we going to stay there tonight?" Eliezer asked.

"We'll have to," Gershom replied. "It has the only well around here."

That night Zipporah lay awake, musing about the past and wondering about the present. *At this place the Lord spared Moses from death. Surely He will continue to protect my husband.* "Tell me, Lord," she pleaded. "Let me know."

She listened to the measured breathing of her two sons . . . and the sound of a mouse nibbling at grains of wheat that had fallen on the floor. Outside in the courtyard a camel grumbled and belched. At last she slept.

In the morning they continued on the flat desert route south. As they journeyed, Zipporah longed for the mountains of home—away from this awesome expanse of land and its overwhelming silence broken only by the creak of saddles and faint padding of the camel's cushioned soles on the sand.

But when we finally reach our tribe, what will they think of me? she wondered. *Maybe like the Ishmaelite leader they'll claim that Moses deserted me.*

To quiet her troubled thoughts, she reached into a saddlebag for her flute. As she played, the wistful melodies floated into the still air.

Suddenly Gershom shouted, "There's a dust storm

whirling toward us from the west."

She glanced around the flat desert. "No hills to find shelter behind!" Quickly they ordered the camels to kneel and then crouched behind them a few seconds before the blowing sand hit. Zipporah drew a blanket from a saddlebag and held it over her face. The camels turned their heads away from the wind and closed their eyes and nostrils. The sand continued to pelt them until Zipporah could feel the weight of it covering her robe.

As suddenly as the storm had arrived, it ended. They shook the sand from their clothes and brushed it from the camels' shaggy coats.

The next morning the trail passed down into a wadi. As the camels carried Zipporah and her sons around a wide bend, a caravan became visible. "Mother," Gershom whispered, "we should turn back."

"It's too late and besides there's no place to hide. We'll have to meet them."

They watched the caravan advance slowly toward them. "It looks like a strange tribe of Midianites," Gershom observed.

"Praise the Lord, they are not Amalekites. I will greet them and pray that they give us safe passage." She pushed her camel past her sons, and then stopped, her heart pounding.

The leader halted his camel and fixed his gaze on her. A sudden vision of a leopard on a trail passed through her mind.

"Peace," she offered.

"Peace," he replied in a cold tone. "Who are you and why are you passing through our territory?"

"I am Zipporah, daughter of Jethro of the Kenite tribe of Midian. These are my two sons Gershom and Eliezer. We are returning to my father. Will you allow us safe passage?"

He glanced beyond her. "Where is the rest of your caravan?"

ZIPPORAH

"We have no others traveling with us."

The leader stroked his beard. "These are strange times when a woman travels alone with only her two sons. If you are from the Kenite tribe, why do your sons have foreign names?"

Zipporah felt her anger rising. *If I were a man, this Midianite would not ask these impolite questions. But to gain safe passage, I'll have to answer.* "My husband named our sons."

"Who is your husband?"

"He is Moses of the Hebrew tribe of Levi."

"Moses!" the man exclaimed. "I've heard of him. Two days ago we passed Ishmaelites who had just come from Egypt. They brought amazing news. This man Moses caused a plague so that the water in the great river Nile turned to blood. Is that not strange?"

Now I know that Moses is alive and doing the will of the Lord, she said to herself. *My prayers are answered.* Aloud she spoke confidently. "My husband is a man whom the Lord has blessed."

The Midianite looked from her to Gershom and Eliezer. "I will give the sons of Moses and their mother safe passage through my territory. Go in peace."

"The sons of Moses and I are grateful."

The leader raised his hand and signaled for the caravan to continue on its way.

Gershom sat tall and expressionless until the last camel had passed. Then, relaxed and smiling, he said, "Since I am the leader of our caravan, I will signal to proceed."

At the end of the wadi a wide white plain sprinkled with red pebbles spread before them. Zipporah gave a joyful cry, "I see the tops of mountains in the distance. We're coming to the great cliffs." In the late afternoon they stood at their brink. Below them the granite mountains, range after range, stretched to the horizon. Zipporah recognized the familiar shape of Mount Horeb far to the south.

"Let's ride down right now," Eliezer shouted.

"Here we must walk," his mother cautioned. "It's too steep to ride." They dismounted and urged the camels toward the trail. The male snarled at Gershom and tried to bite him.

"I'll take the female first," Zipporah said. "Perhaps then yours will come too." The beast whined and complained but finally followed her. The larger camel let out a bellow before it stepped onto the trail.

By the time they cautiously descended, the sun had sunk behind the mountain tops, and complete shadow brought the beginning of the night's chill. A short way into a narrow valley, they found a lone acacia tree, but no water. "We'll have to stop anyway," Zipporah said. "It's too late to look for a spring."

As she was packing the camels the next morning, she noticed a familiar inscription on a boulder. Dashing to the big rock, she ran her fingers over the design. "It's a mallet," she called to Eliezer and Gershom.

They ran to the boulder and touched the inscription. "It's ours!" shouted Eliezer. "It marks the edge of our territory, doesn't it?"

"Now all we need to do is find the tribe," Gershom said.

Their mother nodded. "They should still be camped at Mount Horeb this time of the year."

Three days later they hurried their camels through the narrow pass to the plain in front of the mountain. Gershom halted his camel. His mother rode up beside him and stared at the deserted camping place.

Eliezer was the first to speak. "Where is everybody?"

"Gone," Gershom sighed. "They've already left for the copper mines."

Before sleeping, Zipporah checked the remaining supply of food—a handful of parched wheat, enough barley for one meal, a few raisins . . . nothing more.

Continuing their journey south they traveled as far and as fast as they could each day. Their food soon ran out. Exhausted from the long rides with only camel milk to sustain her for two days, Zipporah lay down on a sheepskin next to a thorny bush covered with lavender blossoms.

A bee gathering nectar from the flowers buzzed close to her ear. Cautiously she opened her eyes and watched the bee dart away to a rocky hillside. She stood up and wrapped a shawl firmly around her head, leaving only a slit for her eyes. With a knife and a bowl in her hands she walked toward the rocks.

Humming a gentle tune to warn the bees of her approach, she proceeded slowly until she found a large honeycomb hidden in the rocks. Still humming, she cut pieces from it and dropped them into her bowl.

The bees circled angrily around her head but were unable to attack her through the heavy shawl. One landed on her hand, its sting a dart of fire. She brushed the insect away and stood completely still until the others became more calm. Then she walked slowly away from the rocks. The swarm followed, still trying to attack her head until she was nearly at the camp. Abruptly they left and returned to their hill.

Her hand had begun to swell. She paused to spread honey onto it, soothing away the pain as her mother had done when she was a child.

Eliezer ran to meet her. "Gershom and I found some quail eggs."

She smiled at him. "Good! I brought honey."

"Can I have some now?"

She cut off a piece of honeycomb and handed it to him.

"If you and Gershom gather some wood for the fire, I'll roast the eggs."

Eliezer dashed back to the camp and yelled at his brother, "Come on, let's find some wood."

After starting the fire, Zipporah poured water on the ground. Then covering the eggs with a thick coat of mud, she placed them into the fire. By the time she finished milking the camel, the eggs had baked.

Raising her head, she looked at the sky.

Eliezer licked his lips. "Let's eat."

Gershom placed his hand on the boy's shoulder. "Wait a minute. I think Mother is going to pray."

"Thank you, Lord," she said, "for eggs and honey and milk. Once again You have provided."

The next day they noticed sheep tracks along the trail.

Gershom studied the marks. "They're fresh. The wind hasn't blown sand over them yet."

Zipporah felt strength returning to her tired body. "If we ride late tonight, we might be able to catch up with the tribe."

By the time the sun set, the tracks led into a valley but still they saw no sign of the Kenites. The little caravan rode on. The sky darkened and stars came out. A full moon rose.

"Stop," said Zipporah. "I think I hear sheep." They listened. The unmistakable sound of ewes calling to lambs drifted down to them.

"Let's go," Eliezer urged.

A jumble of boulders showed dark to one side of the trail. From among the rocks a harsh voice demanded, "Who is invading Kenite territory?"

Moonlight glinted off the raised spear in his hand.

Chapter 14

Hobab! It's your sister with Gershom and Eliezer."
He lowered the spear. "Zipporah?"
"Yes. We have returned."

Other men appeared from behind boulders. "Jethro's daughter has come back to her tribe."

Standing beside her camel, Hobab asked, "Where is Moses?"

"His brother came to meet him, and they continued on to Egypt." She leaned down and touched his shoulder. "And now my brother has come to meet me."

He walked ahead of the camels to the silent camp and Jethro's tent. "My father's tent," Zipporah said softly. "I'm home."

She saw the old man rise from his rug by the fire. "Hobab, who is with you?" he asked.

"Zipporah and your grandsons have returned."

Jethro came forward to embrace them. "Welcome home, Daughter and Grandsons." Her father peered into the darkness. "Where is Moses?" Zipporah sighed. "He continued on to Egypt."

"Of course," the old priest replied. "I must not forget

112

that the Lord called him for a great purpose."

Jamila came from the women's end of the tent. "How did you manage to get here without your husband?"

"He arranged for me to travel with Ishmaelites, but I decided to leave them." She hugged her sister. "Even with the camels I bought, it was a hard journey, but now I'm home to Father's tent. Do you sleep here? I thought Misha and her family lived with Father."

Before Jamila could answer, Jethro spoke in a hushed voice. "Two moons ago Achmaz went to his forefathers. When Azaz became our new leader, he moved his family into his own tent again. Jamila takes care of me now."

"So Misha is the wife of the leader," Zipporah murmured in wonder. "Our Misha."

"You can greet your sisters in the morning," he directed. "Sleep now. Come, Grandsons. I will share my sheepskins with you."

Carrying a saddlebag, Zipporah followed her sister into the tent. Before lying down she rubbed her hands on a ewe's wool to feel the soothing lanolin, to savor its familiar smell. Then breathing in contentment, she fell asleep.

When the first pastel colors lightened the sky, Zipporah stepped outside to relish the early morning . . . to listen to the sound of sheep hooves on rocky soil and the running feet of a child returning from a trip to the bushes . . . to smell smoke from a cooking fire and the pungent odor from a clump of oregano.

Fara was the first sister to find her. Then others arrived, and finally Misha. The two eldest daughters faced each other in silence until Misha proudly announced, "I am the wife of the leader."

"You will do well," Zipporah replied.

Her sister's expression showed no emotion. "So Moses

grew tired of you and sent you home."

"If that's what you think, I won't try to explain."

"I suppose you'll look for a new husband now that yours has left you."

Zipporah stepped back. "Moses will return. I'll wait for him."

"In the meantime don't look at my husband," Misha said before she stalked away.

Will she ever trust me? Zipporah wondered.

After a few days the tribe continued on its way to the copper mines. Zipporah settled into the familiar routines, helping wherever needed during shearing and lambing. Some of the women avoided her, inferring that because her husband had sent her home, she was not welcome to visit in their tents.

All this time Azaz gave no indication that he was aware of her return, never once looking directly at her. Then one evening as she was drawing water from a well, he stood beside her. "No Midianite woman should live without a husband. If Moses doesn't return within a year, I shall declare him dead and take you into my tent as my second wife."

She shrank away from him. "No!"

His smile was cold. "If you refuse, I will banish you and your sons from the tribe."

Grabbing the water bucket, she ran toward her father's tent. Azaz' harsh laughter followed her. Inside she fell trembling onto a rug.

When the tribe had finished trading wool for copper, its chieftain leader raised his hand to signal that they must resume their migration. The caravan journeyed south along the sea. Zipporah took deep breaths of the fresh breeze, but her eyes turned often to the western mountains. Far beyond them Moses was fulfilling his commission from the Lord.

Moons waxed and waned. Ishmaelite caravans brought news from Egypt. "Frogs cover the land." "Horrible plagues of lice and fleas." "Those Israelite slaves want freedom but Pharaoh refuses to let them go." "Cattle die—even the sacred bulls." "That Hebrew who used to live with your tribe is stirring up all this trouble."

"When's Father going to return?" Eliezer demanded to know.

His mother reassured him. "As soon as he can." Silently she added, I *pray he will come before a year has passed.*

Fewer caravans arrived from the west. "We stay away from Egypt as much as possible," one trader told Jethro. "There's too much abomination in that land."

Many nights Zipporah lay awake. If she didn't meet his demand, would Azaz really banish Gershom and Eliezer along with her?

Only one moon remained in the year. As the tribe headed toward some palm trees that marked a camping place, Jethro called, "I see a tribe of Ishmaelites. If they've come from Egypt, we'll have news."

As soon as they dismounted, Zipporah followed her father to the Ishmaelite camp. While he and the leader inquired into each other's health, she waited impatiently. Finally Jethro remarked, "Perhaps you have come from Egypt."

The leader looked up to the sky. "God forbid that I should ever have to witness such a plague again. Thick darkness covered the land for three days. As soon as I could see, I took my caravan out of Egypt. We left before the most terrible plague of all."

"Something more terrible than complete darkness?" the old priest prompted.

Holding his hand over his eyes, the leader said, "Since I left, I've heard that because Pharaoh refused to let the Israelites leave, there was death for all Egyptian firstborn. Every firstborn—even Pharaoh's son."

"What about the Hebrews?"

"There was no death for these that call themselves Israelites. They were passed over. That man Moses is now leading them with all their flocks and herds across the southern wilderness. They're almost to Mount Horeb."

Zipporah had heard enough. She struggled to a palm tree and sank onto the sandy soil. It saddened her that because of Pharaoh's stubbornness, all the firstborn had to die. Her eyes filled with tears of sympathy for Egyptian mothers.

But now at last Moses was leading his people to the mountain. A great longing to be with him washed over her.

When Jethro walked toward her, she stood up. "Father, I must go to my husband. Will you take me to him? If he's not already at the mountain, I'll wait for him there."

He paused so long that she wondered if he had heard. At last he answered. "Two days from now, we will go to the mountain."

Once again she and her sons must leave the tribe, but this time they would have camels to ride and donkeys to carry the tent and other equipment.

As she began to pack saddlebags, five of her sisters entered the tent. Tuema's voice revealed sadness. "So we have to say goodbye again."

"And this time perhaps it is forever," Duhiya added.

116

Fara put her arms around her oldest sister, "Oh, Zipporah, how can we let you go?"

Jamila glanced out the tent's open side. "Here comes Misha."

The five sisters shrank back toward the tent walls as Misha stood defiantly in front of Zipporah. "So you are deserting me again."

Zipporah shook her head. "You don't need me now that you are the leader's wife."

"You're wrong! I do need you."

Zipporah frowned, puzzling over what her sister meant. "Jamila takes care of Father. Why do you need me?"

"Now that I'm the leader's wife, the women are afraid of me." Misha's gaze took in the other sisters. "Look, even they avoid me. You're the only one who is not afraid."

"That's because I'm older and you always had to do what I asked."

Tuema stepped closer. "I remember when you always told Misha to keep her throwstick ready."

"Yes," Tarfah added, "and how you both protected us when the shepherds invaded."

Misha spoke directly to Zipporah. "I haven't forgotten that you saved my son's life the night he was born." She paused. "Just think of all the years I've wasted arguing with you."

"I'll miss you," whispered Zipporah. "I'll even miss our arguments."

They clung together for a few moments. Then Misha walked slowly away, head held high as befitted the chieftain's wife. The other sisters hugged Zipporah. Watching them follow Misha, she questioned silently, *After tomorrow will I ever see them again*? She glanced at the tents. Or *anyone from this tribe*?

ZIPPORAH

The next day's journey to the mountain seemed longer than usual to Zipporah. Overcome with eagerness, she fretted at the slow pace of the animals. Late afternoon sunshine splashed golden tones on the red mountains before Jethro turned into the narrow pass. Part way through, he suddenly halted his camel. Zipporah glanced up. Above them on boulders, a group of men enclosed the small caravan. Bronze-tipped spears flashed in each man's right hand.

"Who are you and why are you entering the pass to Mount Horeb?" one man demanded.

"I am Jethro of the Kenite tribe of Midian. I am taking my daughter to her husband."

"Who is her husband?"

"Moses. The leader of the Israelites."

The man was silent for a moment before he asked, "Who are these other two?"

"Moses' sons."

"How do I know this is true? They are dressed like Midianites."

Gershom spoke up. "We are wearing Midianite robes but like our father, my brother and I are Hebrews."

"Will you take a message to Moses?" Jethro asked. "Tell him that I am bringing his wife and sons to him."

"Wait here," the man replied. "I will deliver the message." He climbed down from the boulder and disappeared along the narrow pass. The other men lowered their spears.

"This close," Zipporah said to her father, "and yet we must wait to enter a part of our own Kenite territory."

"We will get off our camels and rest awhile," the old man answered. "Moses will come for us soon."

A small, wistful sound escaped from her throat. "It's been so long since I've seen him."

ZIPPORAH

Sunlight was fading from the mountaintops when she heard footsteps, and Moses stood before her, his tall figure appearing even bigger than she remembered. Jethro embraced him. They inquired into each other's health, but Moses' gaze turned often to his wife and his sons.

Unable to wait any longer, she stepped forward and then his arms were around her. She laid her face against his broad shoulder while he held her tightly, resting his cheek against her head.

This is really home, thought Zipporah. *This is where I belong—in my husband's arms.*

After greeting Gershom and Eliezer, Moses led the way toward the mountain. When at last they rode out of the pass, Zipporah gasped at the scene before her. Never had she seen another tribe at the sacred camping place, and now men, women, children, sheep, and cattle covered the plain. Cooking fires sent up curls of smoke. Children yelled. Sheep pushed at each other as they grazed on the meager amount of grass.

"Aaron's and my tent is nearby," Moses announced. Through its open side Zipporah saw a women patting out thin, flat cakes of a strange dough. Was she Aaron's wife? Or had Moses taken a second woman during their long separation? Zipporah's voice was a faint whisper. "Who is she?"

"My sister Miriam. The Lord has commissioned her to lead the people along with Aaron and me. Come now and meet her."

Miriam, she said to herself. *At last I can meet the sister who watched over Moses when he was a baby and who told him about the one true God.*

The older woman's voice was cool. "Is this the foreign woman you married?"

"She is no longer foreign," Moses insisted. "We have a

marriage covenant, and I want you to treat her as a member of our tribe."

"She doesn't look like a Levite. Her skin is darker than mine."

Moses drew a deep breath. "You will treat her with respect."

Without answering, Miriam went into her room. Zipporah drooped with disappointment. *She doesn't like me. I was so sure I would love her and I had hoped that she would accept me.*

Her husband's words broke into her thoughts. "We've been parted too long. Are you all right? Did the Ishmaelites treat you well?"

"When they decided to go to Damascus, we left their caravan at the northern mountain."

His mouth opened in shock. "How could you travel across the wilderness without the donkeys?"

She smiled. "I bought camels."

"I don't see how you made it safely home."

"When I thought of my tribe's tents, that's where I wanted to be."

He took both of her hands in his. "That's where you wanted to be, but now I'm asking you to leave your homeland forever. Do you want to go? Once we start out, there will be no turning back."

"Of course I want to go. I belong to your tribe, and wherever you are, that now is home to me."

"There will be fighting with pagan tribes before we reach Canaan." He dropped her hands. "You'll be safer if you and Eliezer return to your father's tent. Gershom can go with me. We will send for you and the boy after we enter the land."

Chapter 15

Before she could object, a noisy group of men filled the opening to the tent. "We are from the tribe of Benjamin," a man shouted, "and those Simeonites have claimed some of our cattle."

Moses walked heavily away to settle the dispute.

While he was gone, Zipporah led the donkeys to the edge of the camp where she found a place to set up her tent. Two Israelite women eyed the brown and white robe she was wearing and then whispered to each other. One stepped closer. "We will help you pitch your tent."

Zipporah glanced at the tightly-woven linen that the woman wore. "Thank you. I am grateful for your help." After they had fastened the last rope to a stake and raised the final pole, she carried sheepskins and blankets into the room where Moses, Jethro, and her sons would sleep. With that accomplished, she arranged her chamber. *Our tent*, she reflected. *All those years when we cared for Father, we lived in his tent. Now at last we have our own home again.*

Jethro settled in for a visit with Moses. During the evening meals Zipporah listened while the two men sat by the fire and talked. Gershom and Eliezer savored every

121

word—how their father and uncle went before Pharaoh and demanded that he let the Israelites leave Egypt, how the Lord sent terrible plagues, how the Red Sea parted to allow the people to walk safely to the other side, how they celebrated the Passover.

Too often, however, the men had their conversations interrupted when someone came with a complaint, a problem, or a demand for help. Then Moses would leave his unfinished supper and go out to take care of the peoples' needs.

A moon passed . . . and another. Time and again Moses climbed the mountain to talk to the Lord.

As Zipporah went about her daily chores—walking to a spring for water—milking a camel or a ewe—she heard the people grumble, "Why don't we leave this place and go to Canaan?"

One day as she gathered brush for her fire, Miriam walked toward her with a determined stride. Zipporah admired her sister-in-law's straight and regal posture. Surely she looked like the prophetess that she was—a chosen one—a leader like her brothers.

The older woman confronted Zipporah. "Your father is interfering. He's been telling Moses how to rule our people, even suggesting that he appoint extra judges." Her voice rose. "All this takes too much time."

"My father is a wise man," Zipporah answered humbly.

"I don't think he's so wise. Why doesn't he go back where he came from?"

Zipporah didn't answer, but her mind raced ahead. *When he leaves, Eliezer and I will have to go with him.*

That evening when her father and Moses arrived for the evening meal, Jethro announced, "Tomorrow morning I will return to my tribe."

His daughter placed her hands over her mouth to stifle

a cry. *Don't take me away. Leave me here with my husband.*

"Go in peace," Moses said. "As I have mentioned, I would like to send my wife and Eliezer to you until it is safe for them in Canaan. But since your tribe is camped only a one-day journey away, I will wait. I can easily take them to you when the time comes for me to leave Midian."

Jethro nodded. "My eldest daughter and my grandson are welcome in my tent at any time."

Trying to blot out her fears, Zipporah closed her eyes.

The next morning her father mounted his camel. "I will see you soon," were his last words to her before she watched him ride away.

As the days passed, she often stopped to rest and ponder how she could help her husband. Although he now had leaders for settling some of the Israelites' disputes, he still appeared tired. One evening as she massaged his tense shoulders, he said, "Tomorrow I will go up the mountain."

"Again? Why do you have to go up there so often?"

"I always need to know what to do next."

From the other side of the fire Eliezer asked, "Why can't I go with you sometime?"

Moses looked fondly at the boy. "I've told you before that it's not safe. I'm sorry, Son. I must go alone."

"We need to stay here and take care of the camels and donkeys," Gershom tried to calm his little brother.

During the night Zipporah woke up several times. Of course it wasn't safe. Although the mountain was beautiful and holy, it was an awesome and fearful place when God came down to meet with Moses.

Just before daybreak when she heard footsteps, she threw back her blanket and hurried into the center room. It was empty. Running to the tent's open side, she saw her husband's tall figure as he strode toward the mountain, now covered with somber shadows. She pulled her robe more tightly around her shoulders and stood shivering in the pre-dawn chill.

As she saw Miriam look out of her tent, Zipporah felt an impulse to run and hide, but it was already too late. Her sister-in-law came to stand beside her. They watched Moses walk across the valley and begin the long climb.

Miriam's accusing voice broke the silence. "He should take Aaron and me with him. I suppose you tell him to go alone."

Zipporah shook her head.

"I don't tell my husband what to do."

"Your father certainly didn't hold back any advice. Moses should have consulted with Aaron and me, not with a foreigner."

Zipporah had also wondered why he didn't share more responsibility with his sister and brother. The Lord had chosen them also to serve as leaders. Remaining silent, she watched Moses as he climbed up the ravine.

From the mountaintop a low rumble drifted down to the camp.

The thunder-like reverberation continued the next day. Zipporah glanced often at the mountain, searching for a sign of her husband. She found it difficult to concentrate on her tasks.

"Mother, you look worried," Gershom commented. "I wish I could go up and look for Father."

"Me, too," Eliezer added.

"Of course you can't go," she exclaimed. "No one must even go near or touch the mountain these days when the Lord speaks with your father."

Sudden lightning struck at the high rocks. She screamed and clapped her hands over her ears to shut out the deafening thunder. Through a driving hailstorm, she saw Moses working his way down the rugged slope.

He appeared tired but not dazed as he had been long ago when the Lord had first spoken to him. While he rested, she washed his feet and then rubbed his forehead with warm sesame oil. *When the time comes to go back to my father,* she asked herself, *will some other woman want to wash his feet and rub oil on his forehead? Someone needs to care for him. I want that one to be me.*

When the time comes, still echoed in her mind a few days later as she walked to a spring in a nearby wadi. A slight sound from behind a boulder caused her to pause. *Probably just a small rodent,* she thought, *or maybe a quail.*

Without warning a man's hand reached from behind the boulder and grabbed her arm.

"Azaz! What are you doing here?"

"Don't scream," he ordered. "I want to talk to you."

"If you let go of my arm, I'll listen."

He relaxed his grip but still held her wrist.

She stared into his hostile eyes. "How did you get past the Israelite guards?"

"Ha!" he laughed. "Have you already forgotten that I've lived in these mountains all my life? I know every twist and turn, every passageway. These men were mere slaves in Egypt. What do they know about guarding a camp?" His fingers tightened on her arm. "Why is your husband invading Kenite territory?"

"He's only passing through on the way to Canaan."

"So you say," he hissed, "but he's a long way from the main caravan route."

As calmly as possible she replied, "The Lord has led him here."

"The Lord may have led him here, but my armed men can drive him out."

Trying to pull away from him, she faltered, "Your armed men?"

"You don't think I would come here alone, do you? I have all my men hidden among the rocks. We are ready for the attack." Rubbing his hand up her arm, he pulled her toward him until her face was close to his. His voice was low and smooth. "And after I drive these Israelites out of my territory, you're going to return to my tribe with me."

She twisted away from his grasp. "Why do you want me to go with you?"

"I told you before you married that Hebrew, you are not loyal to your tribe. No Midianite woman should leave her people."

Trying to keep her voice steady, she backed away from him.

"I will not go with you."

"Don't try to escape," he growled. "You got away from me when you married Moses, but this time I will have you." He grabbed her arm again. "I'll leave two of my men to guard you while the rest of us attack."

Once more she tried to pull away, but he was too strong for her. With trembling voice she choked out the words, "You cannot fight against the Israelites. It's against Kenite tribal law."

"How so?" he demanded.

"Long ago when my father made a blood covenant with Moses, he and all his family were guaranteed safe passage in your territory. You were there and I heard you say, 'So be it.'"

Azaz scowled. "I remember safe passage for Moses and his family, but not for this multitude."

"This multitude is his family," she cried. "They are the children of Israel."

He slipped a dagger from his belt and pointed it toward her throat. "There are too many of them. They need to be cut down."

She shrank back. "Kenite law is unbreakable even by the leader."

"Achmaz would never have allowed this invasion."

"Even Achmaz obeyed the law."

Azaz jerked her closer. Not daring to resist, she waited. For several moments he stared at the dagger, then with a sigh replaced it in his belt. "So be it." Glaring at her, he added, "You have joined yourself to a strange people."

"They are my people now."

Abruptly he shoved her away. "They can have you." Motioning to his men hidden behind high rocks, he strode away.

Quickly Zipporah raced toward her tent. With relief she saw Moses sitting at the entrance. "Azaz and his fighting men," she said breathlessly. "They were ready to attack."

He stood. "Where did you see him?"

"On the way to the spring. Azaz tried to force me to go with him. He even threatened me with his dagger."

Fierce anger blazed in her husband's eyes. "I will never allow any man to attack my wife or my people." He glanced around for his warriors. Shouting orders to Joshua—his second in command—he dashed toward the center of the camp. A trumpet sounded and armed men raced toward the spring.

Zipporah ran to Moses. "Wait. Azaz is gone. I reminded him that you have safe passage—you and your family, all the children of Israel."

Her husband faced her with a puzzled look. "And Azaz agreed that we have safe passage in his territory?"

"It's Kenite law, and laws must not be broken," she answered. "No Midianite of the Kenite tribe, even a cruel man like Azaz, would ever break a covenant."

"My warriors will still make sure that the camp is well

guarded." Together they walked back to the tent. "You're trembling."

With his arms around her, she leaned her head against his shoulder. "I never want to return to the Kenites. I'm ready to go with our tribe—yours and mine—to the Promised Land."

For a long moment he held her in his arms before he said, "You're a courageous woman. How could I have considered leaving you with your father?" He looked at her with deep admiration. "I'm sorry I have to be gone for awhile."

"Does that mean you're going up the mountain again?"

"Yes, I have to learn more about what the Lord wants the people to do. He's promised to give laws and a new covenant for us."

"When will you come back?"

"I'm not sure. I only know that this is the day He has called me to go."

She grasped his arm with both of her hands. "I'm afraid for you to to up there." A sob escaped from her throat. "When the mountain rumbles, it might send rocks down on you."

Moses put his arms around her again, and held her in a warm embrace. "Don't be afraid. I'll come back."

She walked with him to the tent's open side and managed to give him a pensive smile. "From now on, I'll remember that when the Lord calls, you must go."

Kissing her gently, he turned toward the mountain of God.

Gershom and Eliezer came to stand beside their mother. They watched their father cross the plain to enter the ravine. Slowly he climbed upward.

High above, sunshine touched a bright cloud that covered the mountaintop.

GUIDEPOSTS

Huldah

Lois Erickson

CARMEL • NEW YORK 10512

This book was
Edited by Richard W. Coffen
Designed by Helcio Deslandes
Cover art by John Edens
Typeset: 11/13 Novarese Medium

PRINTED IN U.S.A.

R&H Cataloging Service
Erickson, Lois N. (Lois Nordling), 1920-
    Huldah.

    I. Title.
        221.9

ISBN 0-8280-0671-7

Chapter 1

Huldah, daughter of Barak, smiled as she made her morning plans. Her father had given her enough silver beads to buy a length of linen for a summer robe. Peeking out of her room, she glanced at the partially enclosed cooking area and other rooms that surrounded the small courtyard. Seeing neither her mother nor the maidservant, Kezia, nor the gatekeeper, Samuel, she slipped out quickly and pulled open the solid sycamore gate that led to the street.

She wore a green woolen robe that reached to the top of her tan leather sandals. A soft, cream-colored shawl, embroidered with yellow and orange yarn, covered her head and long brown hair. The silver beads rested comfortably in a small pouch she had tucked into a wide sash at her waist.

Already at this early hour the people of Jerusalem were leaving their homes and heading toward the noisy marketplace. Huldah pulled the large shawl more snugly around her shoulders. The street was a narrow canyon

5

twisting between high stone walls, and the sun had not yet reached down to warm the passageway.

A short distance from her father's house, she could hear the merchants in the market shouting out their wares. She turned into the open section of mud-brick stalls where vendors sold food and peddlers spread their merchandise on the wide cobblestone street.

"I have a fine grade of almonds for you to buy," a shopkeeper called to her.

Huldah shook her head.

"Olive oil, pure olive oil," shouted the owner of the next shop.

She ignored him and continued in the direction of the linen merchants' street. Suddenly she stopped. Ahead of her at a grain seller's stall a young man in a brown robe was inspecting a basket of wheat. She frowned. She had seen this same man in the marketplace for the past three days. Not only loitering in the streets but watching her. Although she was accustomed to men's admiring glances, this man's presence annoyed her. Was it because he looked at her not with admiration but with curiosity?

To avoid him she turned into the street of basketmakers. Here baskets woven from palm fronds, reeds, or willow branches hung on the shops' walls and from ropes across the top of the narrow street.

Huldah pushed through the crowds of shoppers and into the street of clothing and fabric merchants, stopping at a linen shop. Mud-brick walls supported wooden beams for the closely-packed mud roofs. Three steps led up to the stone floor, and along the walls lengths of colorful linen hung from wooden rods.

"Welcome, welcome." The shopkeeper bowed to her. "You've come to buy at a time when the selection is at its best. Last week an Egyptian ship arrived in Joppa, and a caravan brought the linen to Jerusalem just two days ago."

Huldah fingered a white piece with an elaborate border in shades of yellow, orange, and red. A robe-length of blue linen drew her attention—until she caught sight of the young man in the shop across the way. *He's just pretending to examine that pair of sandals,* she thought. *He's really watching to see what I'm buying.*

The proprietor of the linen shop reached for the blue piece and waved it in front of her. "I can give you a good price for this one."

She shook her head. "Thank you. I'll not decide today."

Still waving the blue, he followed her into the street. "Look at this fine weaving. What will you offer?"

How can I concentrate on a piece of fabric when a man is following me around the marketplace? Huldah thought.

"I'll not decide today," she repeated.

Muttering a few angry words, he returned to his shop.

With determined steps, Huldah left the marketplace and hurried along a street toward the mount where the Temple stood. She glanced behind her but saw no sign of the man who had been watching her from the sandalmaker's shop.

The street ended at the top of a cliff. Below she could see the open area where homeless beggars spent the night. A path led across and up to a gate in the retaining wall of the Temple mount, where Solomon's Temple stood tall and majestic. Morning sunshine touched its cream-colored limestone blocks, turning them to gleaming gold.

Gazing at the temple she prayed, "Please, Lord, send us a good king who will remove the altars and statues of Baal from your house of worship."

Just looking at the strength and magnificence of the 300-year-old temple reassured her that someday the Lord would send a good king. She repeated her petition then reluctantly turned away.

As she walked along the winding street that led to her father's house, she wondered if the man in the brown robe was following her. Resolving to find out, she turned a corner and pressed herself against the wall. Shoppers on the way to market passed, and suddenly the man appeared around the corner.

Huldah stepped forward. "Pardon me, sir," she said in her most lofty manner. "Why are you following me?"

His body stiffened in surprise. "I cannot say."

She met the gaze of his dark brown eyes. "You've been watching me in the marketplace."

"Yes, I have."

"Why?"

He rubbed his neatly-trimmed black beard. "I needed to know more about you."

For a moment she struggled to regain her composure. "More about me? What do you already know?"

He stepped closer to her, but she backed away. "I know your name is Huldah. You're 17 years old and live with your father and mother not far from the Temple mount. Your father, Barak, is a scribe, and he has taught you to read and write. I know you come to the cliff every day to look at the Temple."

How did he know all this? What did it mean? She drew in a sharp breath. "Who are you?"

He smiled warmly. "I can't tell you. Not yet." Briefly his smile and his words distracted her, then she ducked past him and ran down the street toward her father's house.

At its high stone wall, she called, "Open the gate." As soon as old Samuel unbarred the heavy wooden gate, Huldah rushed in and slammed it behind her.

Her mother stood in the courtyard. She was a plump

woman. Now anxiety showed on her round face. "What's the matter? Why did you dash in like that?"

Huldah hesitated. Her mother was a chronic worrier, but if Abital couldn't find out the reason for her daughter's hurry, she would imagine the worst possible situation. "It's nothing really, Mother, only that a man in the marketplace was watching me."

"Who is this man?"

"I don't know. I asked him why he was following me, but he wouldn't say."

"You talked to him! It's not proper for a woman to talk to a man, let alone a stranger." Abital's voice rose. "Your father should never have taught you to read and write. That's why you're so bold and strong willed. Just because he has no son doesn't mean he should teach his only daughter."

Huldah stared dutifully at her sandals. "Yes, Mother, I know I shouldn't talk to a stranger, but he made me so angry."

Abital walked to the cooking counter where small loaves of unbaked bread rested on a floured board. "I've told you time and again to take Kezia with you when you go to market."

"When she goes with me, she always says she's tired and that I walk too fast."

"You're just making an excuse," grumbled her mother. "These are evil times in Jerusalem, and a young woman must be on guard." She poked at the loaves to test their readiness for baking. "But what can we expect when we have a corrupt king with a son who is just like his father? The only person in the palace who has any sense at all is Princess Jedidah."

"And her baby, Josiah," added Huldah softly. "Everyday I pray the Lord to send us a good king. Maybe Josiah will become that one."

Her mother sniffed impatiently. "He's only a baby. We'll have a long wait."

"Mother," Huldah confessed, "I didn't get the honey you asked me to buy."

"If you hadn't stopped to talk to that man, you'd have remembered. Now Kezia and I will have to get it when we go out."

Huldah looked around the courtyard for the maidservant. "Where is she?"

"Gone to the cistern for water. As soon as she comes back, we'll go to market. I must get ready. You finish the baking."

After her mother left the cooking area, Huldah turned her attention to the beehive-shaped oven in the courtyard. She used a shovel to pull embers into a stone pot before placing the risen loaves in the hot clay oven. Hearing a call from the street, she waited while Samuel let Kezia in.

"Heavy," complained the servant as she set the water jug on the counter. She was a short, stout woman the same age as Huldah's mother, in her service since their girlhood days. Through the many years their relationship had become more like sisters than mistress and maidservant.

Accustomed to Kezia's complaints, Huldah retreated to her room, her place for quiet times. The bed was a comfortable platform against the stone blocks of the wall. A table and a chair sat on the stone floor, and a heavy drape covered part of one wall. She pushed it aside and took a scroll from a hidden shelf. With the precious papyrus in her hands, her heart filled with gratitude to her father for giving it to her. At the risk of his life he had borrowed scrolls, one at a time, from a temple scribe and copied them for her.

How she loved to spend time in this pleasant room, reading the scrolls and pondering their messages. When a warm, sourdough fragrance drifted in from the courtyard, Huldah slid the scroll back into its hiding place. Using a wooden paddle she removed the crusty, brown loaves of bread from the oven.

Just before sunset her father returned from the scribes' quarters, his place of business. A strongly built man, Barak strode into his courtyard. He carried himself proudly, and his thick gray beard bristled with energy. Abital bustled out of the kitchen to stand close to her husband. "A man has been following Huldah around the marketplace."

"What did he look like?"

"Tell him," urged her mother, pushing Huldah forward.

"Well, he was young and . . ." Huldah checked herself. She had almost said that he was young and handsome. That's not what her father wanted to know. "He was young, and he wore a brown robe, . . . and he had a black beard."

Barak shrugged his broad shoulders. "So a man has been following you. What can I expect when I have such a pretty daughter?"

"But this is a strange man whom we don't know," Abital protested. "I've told Huldah again and again not to go out alone in the streets." She squeezed her eyes shut and tightened her lips.

Barak patted his wife's shoulder. "Don't worry. I can handle the situation. Now where's my evening meal?"

Huldah stared at her father. She had expected him to grumble about corrupt times in Jerusalem and even in all the southern kingdom of Judah.

Abital's mouth dropped open in astonishment. "How will you . . ." she began but after a glance at her husband's face, she hurried to the kitchen to set out the soup bowls for supper.

In the room where the family ate, clay lamps on the table cast a warm light. Kezia served cheese, bread, and honey, then brought steaming lentil and onion stew from an iron pot kept hot on the room's hearth. After taking a bowl to Samuel in the kitchen, she seated herself next to Abital.

By the time Huldah carried some lamps to her room, the night had turned dark. A low fire burned on the hearth, and smoke escaped through a high latticed window in the back wall. She was poring over a psalm of King David when a slight knock at the courtyard gate startled her. Strange. Usually a guest or messenger would shout a greeting from the street.

Huldah heard her father unbar the gate and let someone enter. She peered out her door, and in the flickering light of the courtyard torches, she saw the brown-robed man.

Chapter 2

The stranger was holding a bundle wrapped in a dark shawl.

When Barak walked toward her door, Huldah shrank back against the wall. "Come to my room," her father told her in a low voice. "I want you to hear what this man has to say."

Biting her lower lip, she followed the two men into her father's room. "Please explain to my daughter why you are here."

The visitor faced her. "My name is Shallum, son of Tikvah, who lives in southern Judah. I'm assistant to the keeper of the king's wardrobe."

Huldah drew back. What was a man who worked for evil King Manasseh doing in her father's house?

He produced a ring from his leather waistband. "I'm on a secret mission for Prince Amon's wife. Here's the princess' signet ring. To prove that I come in her service, she sent it for you to see."

Huldah stared at the gold ring he held between his

thumb and finger. Deeply engraved on the top were the markings that indicated the princess' name, Jedidah. "Why would she want me to know that you come in her service?"

Shallum returned the ring to a pocket in his leather waistband. "She asked me to find a young woman she could trust, and I have decided that you are the one."

"I don't understand."

"Let the man explain," urged her father.

Shallum took a deep breath. "The princess wants to obey the law of Moses, which says a firstborn son belongs to the Lord. The parents then redeem the child with five shekels of silver. Since Prince Amon worships the false gods Baal and Molech, he refuses to take his son to the priest for this sacred act."

Huldah's voice was a husky whisper. "You mean the baby Josiah?"

"Yes. I've met several times with your father, and we've discussed this situation. For Josiah's sake we must obey the law."

"What am I supposed to do?" Huldah asked anxiously.

"You and I will pose as the baby's parents. Tomorrow morning well before sunrise I'll bring Josiah, and we will take him to a priest at the Temple. The princess will also provide two turtledoves for her own offering of after-childbirth purification." He handed the bundle to Huldah. "She sent this disguise for you to wear."

Her father nodded his head. "Huldah will be ready before sunrise."

Shallum pulled his headcovering forward to conceal his face. "I must go now."

Barak stood up. "I'll unbar the gate."

Huldah remained alone in her father's room. She heard the sound of the men's sandals in the courtyard and the creak of the gate as it opened and closed. With her hands against her forehead to still the turmoil of her thoughts, she sank onto a chair.

Her mother's voice at the door whispered, "I heard what that man said. How could your father allow him to take you into the streets at night?"

Huldah mustered enough courage to say, "We must follow the law the Lord gave to Moses."

"If you're caught, soldiers will kill the baby . . . and you." Her mother stifled a cry. "I worry so much. You're my only child, and I want to keep you safe."

Huldah stood up and put her arms around her mother. *For her sake I'll have to pretend I'm not afraid.* "That man Shallum will protect me."

"You don't even know him. What makes you think you can trust him?"

"Father trusts him, and he knows him better than I do."

With bowed head Abital returned to the courtyard. Back in her own room Huldah opened the bundle. A dark gray robe, rope sandals, a heavy shawl—the clothing of a maidservant. For a long time she lay on her bed, eyes open, staring at shadows flickering on the ceiling from the one torch still burning in the courtyard.

How brave the princess is to obey the law of Moses, she mused. *But how will Shallum find a priest before sunrise?* She pulled her blanket more firmly under her chin. *Can we do all this without Prince Amon or the king finding out that we're taking the baby to the Temple?* "Lord, protect that precious child," she prayed. At last her eyes closed and she slept.

Light and the strong smell from an olive oil lamp awakened her. She heard her mother's anxious voice. "Time to dress."

Huldah rubbed her hand over the coarse fabric of the robe. This was not the type of clothing she usually wore or would ever choose to wear. Quickly she slipped into the dull robe, draped the long shawl over her head, and fastened on the rope sandals. They would make little sound on the cobblestone streets.

A slight knock at the gate made her heart pound. By the light of the lamp in her father's hand, Huldah saw a gray-bearded man in a black robe and black head covering. She drew back toward her room. "Mother, I don't see any baby, and I'm not going with this old man."

Shallum walked quietly across the courtyard. "Don't be frightened," he said. "I have ashes on my beard for a disguise. It would be dangerous if anyone recognized me." He reached into a large pouch that he carried over his shoulder and lifted out the sleeping infant.

Huldah held the warm baby to her shoulder and gently stroked his back. For a moment she closed her eyes, and a shiver passed through her. Is *this really happening*? she wondered. Am I *really holding the future king of Judah in my arms*?

"We mustn't delay," Shallum warned. "We have to complete our mission before he wakes up and cries for his next feeding."

"Where are the turtledoves?"

He patted a smaller pouch.

Huldah frowned at the pouch. "I don't hear them."

"I dropped strong drink down their throats, and they're sleeping."

"Go now," ordered Barak.

Huldah snuggled the baby under her shawl and followed Shallum into the street. In the weak light from a half moon, Huldah could see his shadowy form. Although not as heavily-built as her father, he was taller and had a self-assurance that helped her feel secure. The baby breathed contentedly against her neck.

At each turn of the street, Shallum slowed to watch for

the king's soldiers who patrolled the city at night. When he came to the path that led down into the valley and then up to the Temple mount, he spoke quietly. "Now we have to proceed with extra caution. Soldiers rout out the homeless who try to sleep in the streets and herd them to this valley. All these down here look like beggars, but there might be some of the king's spies among them."

On both sides of the path she could see the dark shapes of the poor. Somewhere a child cried. In Huldah's arms Josiah raised his head. She patted his back, and he settled again with his head on her shoulder.

Where the rocky path wound steeply to a gate in the mount's retaining wall, Shallum took hold of Huldah's hand to lead her up. With the baby cradled in her left arm and Shallum's strong grip on her right hand, for a moment she could imagine that she and this man were wife and husband taking their child to the Temple.

Shallum stopped at the gate, and Huldah dared to ask the question that was bothering her. "Where will we find a priest?"

"As I explained to your father, I've arranged for a priest I can trust to meet us here."

They stood close together outside the bronze gate in the retaining wall. From here they were unable to see the Temple courtyard nor the Temple itself. A wispy cloud drifted across the moon. In the valley all was still.

Soft footsteps announced the arrival of someone in-side, and then the gate opened enough for Shallum and Huldah to slip through. A priest stood in the shadows. A few feet behind him four Temple guards armed with swords and shields waited at attention.

Huldah tightened her hold on the baby. "Can we trust these guards?" she whispered.

"They're employed by the priests," Shallum assured her, "not by the king."

The priest nodded his head in recognition of Shallum, and then asked the ritual question, "What have you brought as an offering to the Lord?"

Shallum lifted the doves from his pouch and handed them to the priest. "We have brought these turtledoves to mark the purification of the child's mother."

He accepted the sleeping doves and slipped them into his robe's inner pockets. "What have you brought to redeem this child?"

"We have brought a bar of silver weighing five shekels. All these offerings we present according to the law that the Lord gave to Moses."

The priest accepted the silver. "And when the child asks why he was redeemed, you will tell him that the Lord slew all the first-born of Egypt but passed over all the first-born descendants of Israel. Then the Lord brought us out of Egypt. Therefore we sacrifice all first-born males of animals, but our sons we redeem."

"We will tell him," Shallum promised.

"Present him for the Lord's blessing."

Huldah removed the shawl from the baby, and Shallum took him into his arms. The priest touched his right hand to the baby's forehead. "This firstborn son is redeemed. May the Lord bless him." He continued to hold his hand on Josiah's head. "Yes, yes," he whispered, "I knew this child's great-grandfather, our good King Hezekiah." He looked up. "But go now. Quickly! I see the beginning of daylight in the eastern sky."

Shallum placed Josiah in Huldah's arms. She held him against her shoulder, and he nuzzled her neck, feeling for milk. Finding none, he whimpered.

Taking her by the hand, Shallum hurried Huldah down

the path and back toward the city. At the first street he paused. "I'll have to leave you here. We can't risk having him cry."

She gave the restless baby to him. Then he and Josiah disappeared into a dark passageway. She turned toward the street that led to her father's house. It too was dark and forbidding, yet faint color in the east warned her to hurry. How safe she had felt when Shallum took her to the Temple mount! Now alone in the silent city she anticipated dangers.

Suddenly she sensed movements. A furry animal brushed past her legs. She sighed in relief. It was only one of the many stray cats that roamed Jerusalem at night, rummaging for food.

As she neared her father's house, the stomp of heavy sandals on the cobblestones indicated a patrol of the king's soldiers. Too late to escape, she curled into the recess of a doorway and pretended to sleep.

The footsteps halted. A big hand reached down and yanked her, sprawling, into the street. "Why are you sleeping here?" a gruff voice demanded. "Take yourself to the beggars' valley where you belong."

By the light of their torches, she looked up into the gleaming eyes of their leader. She raised herself to her knees. "Please, my lord, my benefactor threw me out of his house, but he promised to take me back at daybreak. Could you, my lord, allow me to wait here for him?"

"Absolutely not!" shouted the soldier. "Get up or I'll push you all the way to the valley."

Slowly she stood up, and then behind the patrol another torch appeared. In its light she recognized her father. "Oh, my benefactor," she screamed, "you have come to allow this maidservant back into your house."

"Is this your servant?" the soldier asked.

Barak grabbed her roughly by the arms, "You good-for-nothing female, come with me so I can give you the beating you deserve." He pulled her down the street and into his courtyard, where she collapsed on a bench. He placed the torch in a holder on the wall and then touched her shoulder gently. "When I heard the commotion in the street, I feared for your safety."

"Thank you, Father. I'm grateful you came. The soldiers . . ."

"I heard them, but you're safe now. Did you accomplish what you set out to do?"

Huldah sat up. "Yes. It's done, and I pray that Shallum and the baby are safe also."

"I don't doubt it. He's a resourceful young man."

Abital stepped out of her room. "Are you all right? You look awful."

Huldah rubbed her side where she had fallen against the cobblestones. "Only a few bruised ribs." Thinking of the baby she had taken to the Temple, she added, "I'm fine and all is well."

* * *

Two days later Huldah again evaded her mother and Kezia so she could enjoy a shopping trip to buy the length of blue linen.

As she stood in the marketplace, gazing in at the fabric, the shopkeeper pulled it down from the wall and rushed into the street. "A fine piece of linen this one. The finest!" He held it in front of her. "It's the perfect color for a beautiful young woman like you. The blue sets off your lovely brown hair and eyes. What price will you offer?"

"I'm not sure," countered Huldah. "Perhaps the color is

20

too light." She hesitated, frowning at the fabric. "For what price would you sell it?"

After a lively exchange of words, the shopkeeper agreed to Huldah's final offer. She handed the silver beads to him, and he gave her the linen.

Huldah strolled down the street. No need to hurry now that a man in a brown robe was not following her. Her side still throbbed from the encounter with the soldiers, but it hurt less when she walked slowly.

Entering the crowded street of basketmakers, she considered buying a new basket to hold her sewing. One made of reeds caught her interest, and after bargaining for a price, she placed the blue linen in it.

Strolling again, she looked ahead . . . and into the eyes of a man striding toward her. Was this Shallum in the handsome maroon and white robe? When he stood in front of her, she could smell the sweet fragrance of lanolin and almond oil on his beard.

"At first I didn't recognize you," she confessed.

He chuckled. "I have another message for you from the princess."

Apprehensive, Huldah stared at him without speaking.

"She requests your presence in her chambers tomorrow morning." He paused. "When royalty requests your presence, it's not an invitation. It's a command."

Chapter 3

Huldah clutched her basket tighter and stared at Shallum. "Why? Why does Princess Jedidah want to see me?"

"That is not for me to say."

She searched his face for a clue. His smile told her nothing.

"Tomorrow at mid-morning I will arrive at your father's house to escort you to the palace." Without further explanation, he turned to go.

"Wait! Wait!" She dashed after him, bumping into a vendor and almost dropping the basket. "Have I done something wrong?"

He looked at her sympathetically. "I'm sorry, I can't tell you anything. I'm only allowed to deliver the message."

She watched his striped robe disappear as Shallum wove his way through the crowd.

The next morning Huldah woke up early. She turned restlessly on her bed until she heard Kezia striking a fire at the kitchen hearth. Leaving the bed, she knelt on a rug beside an acacia wood chest, in which her robes and shawls lay neatly folded. *What should I wear to visit the princess?* she wondered. *The yellow with red and orange embroidery? The blue and white stripes?* Finally she chose a sleeveless turquoise robe to wear over her long-sleeved yellow tunic. Orange and yellow embroidery decorated the neckline of the robe as well as the matching shawl. Trying to curb her uneasiness, she wandered around the courtyard. Near the kitchen a mint plant in a clay pot showed its bright green. She crushed a leaf between her fingers and inhaled its sweet fragrance.

"Come, eat some bread," urged her mother.

"I'm not hungry."

"Let her be," ordered Barak.

Abital sighed. "I've instructed Kezia to go with Huldah as chaperon."

"She doesn't need a chaperon to walk with Shallum to the palace," Barak said impatiently. "I wouldn't allow any man to escort my daughter unless I trusted him. He's taking her on a special mission, and Kezia would slow them down."

"I suppose you know what this special mission is?" inquired Abital.

"Shallum has advised me." Barak picked up a pouch that contained his papyrus, ink, and writing reeds to carry them to the scribes' quarters.

Abital sighed again. Huldah turned away to hide her smile. *Dear Father. Once again he has saved me from Mother's overprotection.*

At mid-morning a call came from the street, "Open for Shallum, son of Tikvah." Samuel scuffed across the courtyard to open the gate, and Kezia came to Huldah's door. "That man from the palace is here."

Huldah waited a moment to allow her heart to quiet its

beating before stepping out of her room. Formal and reserved, Shallum stood in the center of the courtyard. He spoke to her quietly, "This is not a secret mission, yet I ask that you follow several paces behind me through the streets, and we must not talk."

"I will do as you request."

In the narrow, twisting street, she hurried to keep up with his long stride. Occasionally he glanced back, but not even a hint of a smile crossed his face.

He led her into the valley and along a causeway paved with rectangular stones. Ahead the road wound up to the wall, high and thick, that surrounded the royal area. Many years before, King Solomon had built this fortified palace on a hill slightly lower than the adjacent Temple mount. At the entrance Shallum shouted, "Open."

"Who is there?" demanded one of the guards inside the wall.

"Shallum, son of Tikvah. By order of Princess Jedidah I have brought Huldah, daughter of Barak."

The gate opened. A palace guard, flanked by six others, scrutinized her and her escort. "You may enter," he said. In the expanse of courtyard that spread toward the huge palace, armed soldiers strolled around or sat in groups, but with eyes alert and weapons near their hands. They nodded in a friendly manner to Shallum and examined Huldah with undisguised interest.

Shallum walked beside her toward an inner wall so high that even the tallest man would be unable to look over. "Miriama will meet you inside the gate of the women's courtyard and take you to the Princess Jedidah."

"Miriama?"

"She's the princess' most trusted attendant." Two guards stood stiffly outside the gate to the women's courtyard. Shallum gave three knocks on the gate. It opened a few inches and a young woman peeked out.

He smiled warmly at her. "I'll wait here while you take Huldah to the princess."

Huldah glanced from Shallum to Miriama and wondered if they were just friends or something more. When the gate behind her closed, she gazed into a garden. Almond trees in full bloom wore clouds of delicate pink and white blossoms. Bright red tulips lined the walks, while beds of white narcissus perfumed the air.

"Come with me," said Miriama. Her rose-colored gown of the finest linen draped softly over her dainty figure. A scarf embroidered with pearls partially concealed shining black hair that fell to her waist. As she walked along the stone path through the garden, she turned her large, expressive eyes to the guest. "What do you think of Shallum?"

Caught by surprise, Huldah searched for an answer. "He's . . . he's very nice."

Miriama stopped under a tree and whispered, "He brought the baby to me that night so I could take him to his mother." Continuing to walk toward the palace, Miriama added, "The princess trusts Shallum. He's of noble birth, son of a chieftain."

No doubt you're of noble birth too, thought Huldah. Jealousy rose within her. *How can I expect Shallum to take notice of me when a beautiful woman of noble birth is interested in him?*

She looked ahead to the cream-colored limestone blocks of the palace. Now so close to her, it was even more massive than she had imagined. Two large Nubian women guarded the entryway. At her surprised gasp, Miriama explained, "Egyptians capture Nubians and export them to other countries. Prince Amon paid a high price for these two at the slave market." The Nubians opened heavy cypress doors.

Inside the women's quarters, Miriama led Huldah down a wide hall and up a stairway to the second level. From somewhere ahead the babble of women's voices invaded the hallway. The ladies of the court! The chatter stopped, and a hush fell over the room when Miriama and Huldah entered.

Many richly-dressed women lounged on soft couches or against cushions heaped on thick carpets. Their gowns were a display of colors, and their sashes vied for length of tassels. Jewelry of gold and precious stones hung around their necks, but most of all Huldah noticed the green copper and black lead cosmetics around the women's eyes. A heavy scent of perfume hovered in the still air—the spicy essence of cassia, the sweet fragrance of spikenard, the clinging aroma of rose.

Scarlet and gold tapestries covered the walls. Bowls of almonds and dates, and platters of rich cakes rested on sandalwood tables. In one corner a dark Nubian woman plucked a harp.

Miriama proceeded across the room to knock at a wide door. "May this one and a guest enter?"

A woman's voice replied, "Enter."

Huldah followed her guide into another large chamber. Miriama closed the door behind them and stood with her back against it. In this room the tapestries were more gold than scarlet, the rugs thicker, the pillow tassels longer.

Dressed in a blue silk gown that reached to the toes of her golden sandals, Princess Jedidah stood before her visitor. Her shawl of darker blue silk hung as long as the gown. Necklaces, bracelets, and the headband that held her dark hair in place were of shining gold. At her feet a sleek tan hound eyed the visitors.

At the sight of the luxurious room and the richly clad princess, Huldah's eyes opened wide in amazement.

Jedidah spoke softly. "Come closer, Huldah, daughter of Barak."

Huldah stepped forward.

"Closer."

Avoiding the side where the hound lay, she advanced again.

"In case someone is listening outside the door, I must speak softly," explained Jedidah. She glanced nervously around the room before continuing. "I want to learn more about the will of the Lord. I know the priests have copies of our history in the Temple, but I'm not allowed to see them. You have copies. Don't ask me how I know. I have ways of finding out such things." She clasped her hands tightly together, and her voice trembled, "I have chosen you to come to my private chambers every day to read to me. My mother told me as much as she knew, but I want to learn more about our ancestors and about the law that the one true God gave to Moses."

Huldah drew a sharp breath but said nothing.

"I can't read the scrolls myself. I don't know how," Jedidah continued. "We must take the utmost care. If the king found out, he could order his soldiers to execute us. To avoid suspicion, most of the day you will conduct a school for the ladies of the court here in these reception rooms. You will teach them to read from Sumerian writings. The king will allow you to use those."

"But I'm too young to teach court ladies," Huldah protested. "I'm only 17 years old."

The princess bowed her head. "I'm only 15, a year younger than my husband. The king arranged my marriage with Prince Amon in order to form an alliance with the chieftains of southern Judah. But I believe God has called me to raise my son so that someday he will serve as a good and faithful king. I need to know more of our history and our law." She hesitated before adding sadly, "I can't read your scrolls to Josiah, but you will teach me how."

The girl's humbleness touched Huldah's heart. "I am honored to become the teacher for you and the ladies of the court."

"I will send Shallum to escort you each day. He and Miriama are the only ones who know of my plan. Everyone else will believe you come to the palace each day only to teach the women." Suddenly she stooped down and touched the hound. It sat up, and she put her arm around its neck. "Do you like my dog? You may pat him."

Huldah hesitated. Touch a dog! The only dogs she had seen were the wild ones that ran in packs outside the city walls.

"Pat him," urged Jedidah. "He won't hurt you. The pharaoh of Egypt sent him to my husband for a wedding present, but Amon hates dogs." She stroked its sleek, short coat. "I don't trust Egyptians any more than I trust Assyrians. Their armies have attacked Judah too many times. But I'm willing to accept this friendly animal."

Huldah reached down and gingerly touched the dog's back. It sat up and gazed at her out of deep amber eyes.

The princess stood and resumed her regal manner. "At each new moon you will receive your wages. Now you are dismissed."

Huldah bowed to the princess and backed to the door where Miriama waited.

At the gate Shallum spoke to Miriama. "I will bring Huldah every day." She smiled sweetly at him before she turned away. He led Huldah to the outside wall and across the causeway to the city streets. All the way her mind raced with questions. Could she safely conceal some writings to carry them to the palace? Was she, a commoner, capable of teaching noble ladies of the court? And not least of all—was Shallum in love with Miriama?

When they returned to her father's courtyard, Shallum warned, "You must take care to tell no one of this arrangement with the princess. As long as King Manasseh pays tribute to the Assyrians so they won't attack Jerusalem, he has ordered the people to worship foreign gods, mainly Baal, Molech, and Asherah." Gently he took her hand in his. "I don't want anything to happen to you."

Glancing into the intent gaze of his dark brown eyes, she managed a low, "I will take care."

Abital emerged from her room with Kezia right behind. "So you have brought my daughter safely home."

Shallum let go of Huldah's hand and stepped away from her. "Yes," he said politely, "and I wish to inform you that Princess Jedidah has chosen her to teach the ladies of the court how to read."

"Oh!" her mother exclaimed. "The princess has chosen her."

"Our own Huldah," said Kezia, "our very own Huldah. The daughter of this household."

Abital smiled up at the tall man standing in front of her. "Did you have something to do with this appointment?"

"After careful consideration, I recommended your daughter to the princess."

"How good of you."

"Each day I will come to escort her to the palace," Shallum explained. He glanced once more at Huldah before he went out the gate.

Abital smiled. "Such a nice young man."

"And so handsome too," added Kezia. "Huldah, I hope you are encouraging him."

* * *

Word spread fast among the gossipers in Jerusalem that Princess Jedidah had chosen Barak's daughter as teacher for the ladies of the court, and that she was using Sumerian writings.

From her scrolls Huldah copied portions on sheets of papyrus, small enough so she could hide them, one at a time, in a pouch under her dress.

Now when Shallum escorted her to the palace, she walked beside him. Always Miriama waited at the gate and exchanged pleasant conversation with Shallum before leading Huldah up the stairways to Jedidah's private chambers on an upper floor. Luxurious rugs, cushions, and couches furnished the rooms. Silk curtains covered the windows. Huldah could hear the voices of the ladies' children playing in a courtyard below.

But her attention centered on the baby Josiah. Propped against a silk cushion while she read and answered questions for his mother, he watched her with his bright eyes, and sometimes he smiled. Other times his head rested against the cushion, and he slept. With its slender chin on its front paws, the pharaoh hound lay nearby.

Huldah listened for footsteps and glanced frequently at the door, imagining she heard soldiers coming to snatch the three of them away to some dark dungeon.

When she left the princess' inner chambers each day to teach the ladies in the reception room, a Nubian brought a chair for her and Sumerian writings from the king's library—books that scholars had translated into Hebrew.

Jedidah sat on a couch, the ladies on plush rugs and cushions. At first her students' frequent giggling and the green and black cosmetics around their eyes distracted Huldah, but soon she thought only of the lessons.

As spring passed, almond blossoms in the garden

turned into green pods. Pink cyclamen and scarlet butter-cups showed their colors. Each time Shallum came to escort her, Huldah yearned for him to touch her hand as he had that first day. But he only led her to the palace and home again. Was it because of Miriama? Or some other reason of which she was not aware? In the street her mind focused on safety. Had the king found out that she was reading to the princess? She looked up at high windows and into passageways. Was an assassin waiting? Would a spear plunge into Shallum's back, and an arrow pierce her heart?

One day the ladies struggled through the words of a Sumerian proverb. "You go and carry off the enemy's lands. The enemy comes and carries off your land." Running footsteps in the hallway and a loud pounding on the door interrupted the lessons.

"Find out what this noise is," Jedidah ordered a slave.

The woman opened the door and a maidservant stumbled in. She fell to her knees and sobbed, "The Assyrians are attacking. They've crossed the northern border of Judah, and they're marching toward Jerusalem."

Chapter 4

The court ladies scrambled to their feet and ran screaming from the room. Jedidah shouted at the maidservant, "How close are they?"

Barely able to speak, the servant croaked, "Almost here." She turned and fled out the door.

"We must stay calm," charged the princess even though her voice trembled. "Miriama and Huldah, come with me to my private chambers." Leading the way into her bedchamber, Jedidah picked up her sleeping son and laid her cheek against his soft dark hair. "My baby, my baby," she crooned. "We won't let the Assyrians harm you."

At the sound of men's voices, Huldah stepped closer to the princess and Josiah. Someone flung open the door and a slender, brown-haired youth rushed in with Shallum following him. Each wore a sword attached to leather waistbands.

"Amon!" cried Jedidah. "We must hide Josiah."

"That's why I'm here. Shallum, prepare the place," he

ordered. "Miriama and . . ." He glanced at Huldah. "You, whoever you are, bring lamps."

Shallum pulled back a carpet and lifted cypress planks from the floor. Amon led the way down a stone staircase into a small room. All descended except Shallum, who waited above to replace the planks and the carpet.

Unable to stand up in the low room, Huldah and Miriama sank onto the thick rug. Prince Amon, fingering his thin short beard, and the princess, with the baby in her arms, sat opposite them. The hound crouched by Je-didah's feet.

"Where will Shallum hide?" Huldah whispered to Miriama.

"He won't. He'll stay with the king's advisors to observe the battle. When it's over, he'll come for us. This is the prearranged plan in case of attack."

"What if . . . what if he can't come?"

A sob escaped from Miriama's throat. "He . . . will. Surely he will come."

The two lamps gave sufficient light for Huldah to see water jugs and baskets of almonds and dates. Large cushions rested on the rug. The prince removed his sword from the scabbard and placed it beside him. "No one will take my son," he growled, "at least not alive."

While Jedidah gradually shifted Josiah to the side away from her husband, Huldah shivered at the thought of what might happen to this baby whom she treasured as if he were her own. No one spoke. The smell of lamp oil hovered in the stale air; only a crack between two stones let in a small amount of freshness.

With her hands over her eyes, Huldah listened for shouts from the courtyards or for the clatter of sword on sword, but the thick walls blocked any sound. *Why are the Assyrians attacking?* she craved to know. *Their empire extends from the Euphrates to Egypt, except for Jerusalem, but Manasseh pays a heavy tribute to their king.*

Jedidah timidly risked the questions. "Why are they attacking?"

Amon's anger flared. "My father refused to pay the latest tribute to King Ashurbanipal."

All fell quiet again. Huldah felt a tightness in her chest. Trying to breathe deeply, she thought of David's prayer as he fled King Saul. *O God, be merciful. . . . In the shadow of Thy wings I will take refuge, till the storms of destruction pass by.*

The wick in one of the lamps sputtered and went out. Amon uttered a short curse, and the baby woke up with a startled cry. While his mother nursed him, the sound of his sucking filled the small room. Huldah stirred restlessly on the rug, trying to picture what was happening outside the city walls, or maybe inside them. Light from the crack between two stone blocks grew dimmer and finally faded into darkness.

Footsteps overhead . . . and then the scrape of wood on wood as someone pulled away the planks. Miriama grabbed Huldah's arm. A lamp cast its glow, and Huldah swallowed in relief to see Shallum standing beside the opening. "The enemy has gone," he announced in a tired voice.

Amon was the first to crawl up the steps. "Gone! Our soldiers defeated them."

"No," replied Shallum. "They used treachery to defeat us and have carried off our king to captivity."

"My father. They've taken my father," the prince cried.

"Tell us how it happened," implored Jedidah.

"Their army surrounded the city, just out of arrow range."

Amon clenched his teeth and hissed, "Our soldiers should have gone out to fight them."

"The Assyrians had the advantage," said Shallum. "We know their bows are stronger and their arrows have a longer range. They sent messengers who promised that their army would not attack if King Manasseh brought the tribute. He and seven officials went out carrying the silver and gold."

"What then," yelled Amon. "Tell me."

"The Assyrians seized the king and the other men, bound them with shackles, and at this moment are marching north."

"We'll ride after them," shouted the prince. "I'll rescue my father."

Shallum shook his head, "Our commanders have advised against it. The enemy's too strong."

Amon reached to the neck of his robe and tore it to the hem. "This never would have happened if my father had allowed me to command his army, but I'm his heir and he thinks he has to protect me." He darted from the room, and Shallum hurried after him.

From the courtyard, women moaned a low wail, the wail of distress for captive men. It wavered through the air and entered the windows of Jedidah's chambers. It spread into the minds and hearts of those listening. Their groans united with it.

When daylight returned, Shallum walked with Huldah to her father's house. Soldiers—spears and bows at hand— crouched on the city wall. No other citizens made their way through the streets. At the gate to Barak's house, Shallum grasped Huldah's hand. "I will come to take you to the palace tomorrow."

His closeness gave her the strength she needed. She smiled at him and wondered about the intense expression in his eyes.

When she entered the courtyard, Abital embraced her

and tearfully sobbed, "You're safe."

Barak patted his daughter's shoulder. "The fortified palace is the safest place during an attack. Even so, those crafty Assyrians used betrayal to capture King Manasseh. I'm not sorry to see him go, except that Amon is worse than his father. What kind of life will we have with that young fool in charge?"

* * *

A caravan of traders journeying from the north brought word that the Assyrians had taken King Manasseh, not to their own capital but all the way to Babylon, a city they controlled. To appease the captors, Prince Amon ordered ten times as many sacrifices of bulls to Baal. The prosperity that the citizens of Jerusalem had enjoyed declined rapidly. With robberies and violence increasing in the city, Barak hired two men to sit outside his gate to guard the household during the night.

Now when Huldah and Shallum walked through the streets, she stayed close to him. In spite of new danger in the city, she cherished these times with her escort. While he dropped handfuls of wheat or barley into beggars' bowls, she waited. If she stopped to feed pieces of bread to hungry cats, he nodded his approval. Occasionally his arm brushed against hers, and his hand rested on her hand.

* * *

By the time Josiah reached his first birthday, he could stand alone, and holding onto the collar of the pharaoh hound, he took wavering steps. "My baby is growing up," the princess said to Huldah, "but I'll soon have another."

Huldah glanced at Jedidah's thickened figure. "Your time's almost here, isn't it?"

"Any day now Josiah will have a brother or sister." She gathered her young son into her arms and cuddled him on her lap. "It's common knowledge that Amon's father burned his firstborn son as a sacrifice to Molech. He threw him into the flames in the Hinnom Valley outside the city wall. If Amon has another son to keep as heir to the throne, he might take Josiah to the Hinnom Valley and sacrifice him to Molech. What can I do?" she cried. "What can I do?"

Huldah knelt by the weeping princess and encircled both mother and baby in her arms. "Can you send him to your family in southern Judah?"

Between sobs the words came. "My mother died when I was born, and now I've received word that my father is gone. I don't know what to do."

Later when Huldah left the princess' chambers, Miriama waited for her in the women's garden and gave a knowing smile. "Shallum is an important man in the palace with many servants working for him. King Manasseh's wardrobe holds more than 2,000 robes and 500 pairs of sandals."

Finding it hard to concentrate after the unnerving conversation with Jedidah, Huldah wondered why Miriama was reviewing this information. The young woman resumed talking. "What do you think of Shallum now that you've known him more than a year?"

What do I think of him? Huldah mused silently. *If only I could trust you, I would confide that I love him. He's not like men who have spoken to my father about me. The caravan leader who said he would burn his firstborn son to Molech. The scribe whom I was afraid might decide to worship Baal. I want a husband who worships God.* Aloud she replied, "He's a kind and thoughtful man."

"Yes, he is." Miriama stopped walking and lowered her

voice. "And he's clever in what he does." Quickly she resumed walking. "I've said more than I should. Please don't repeat it to anyone."

"I won't," said Huldah, trying to keep her irritation from showing. *Miriama is teasing me with these hints of something hidden in Shallum's life. Maybe she's jealous because he walks with me. But she has ways of talking to him in the palace or by the wall that separates the women's garden from the men's.*

Early the next morning a messenger arrived from the palace. "Prince Amon has a new son," he informed Huldah. "The Princess Jedidah requests that while she remains in seclusion, you do not come to teach the women of the court."

As soon as he left, Huldah closed herself in her room. If only the new baby were a daughter, not another son to take Josiah's place in case Amon decides to sacrifice . . . oh, no, no, no! She held her hands over her face to blot out the horrible thought of what could take place in the Hinnom.

Each day she hoped that Shallum would arrive with word of what was happening in the palace. Household activities occupied her time—baking bread, supervising women who came in to do the laundry, marketing with her mother and Kezia; but her thoughts turned often to the remembrance of Shallum's touch to her hand, his arm brushing against hers. Day after day, alternating between hope and dejection, she listened for the sound of his footsteps in the street.

"Why doesn't that nice young man come to see you?" her mother asked. "Just because you aren't going to the palace . . ."

"Huldah, have you been discouraging him?" her father demanded. "I'll never get you married off if you continue to discourage eligible men. I understand why you didn't want to marry the caravan leader, but I don't know why you

38

were disagreeable to that scribe a couple of years ago. I think word got around, and now you've done something to turn this man away."

"No, Father," Huldah protested. "No, I haven't."

Abital broke into the argument. "He's so well thought of in the city, and he has such a good position at the palace."

Barak put his hand over his eyes. "I would welcome a son-in-law who has some money. With King Manasseh in captivity, trade has fallen almost to nothing. That fool Prince Amon ordered a hundred horses, and the Cilicians refused to send them. The rulers of Cilicia don't want silver or gold. They want the linen and wheat we usually buy from Egypt, but we don't have any." He shook his head. "I haven't written a trade contract for two months. No contracts, no orders for goods, and only a few business letters."

"I'm sorry, Father," Huldah hesitated before she continued in a barely audible voice, "I think Shallum is more interested in a noble woman of the royal court than he is in me."

"You mean you've let another woman take him away from you?" Barak asked. "What kind of a daughter have I raised?" He plodded to his room and disappeared behind the door.

Big drops of rain splattered into the courtyard. "Come," said Abital, "we'll help Kezia prepare the supper." In a daze Huldah followed her mother to the kitchen.

Later in her room she drew near to the hearth and warmed her hands at the flame. Rain tapped a gentle rhythm on the courtyard stones. From the street came a call, "Open."

"Who are you?" demanded one of Barak's trusted guards outside the gate.

"Shallum, son of Tikvah."

Huldah heard her father cross the courtyard. "Let the man enter."

Chapter 5

Huldah listened to the tread of Shallum's sandals on the stones as he crossed the courtyard and accompanied Barak into his room. Their muffled voices reached her but were too indistinct for her to distinguish words.

She stared at the floor. *Probably he's talking to Father about the princess. Perhaps, even though her father died, she has decided to send Josiah to her tribe. Would she want me to take him to southern Judah?* Huldah covered her face with her hands. How could she and a little baby survive a journey across the Negev Desert—a place of great whirling winds, of vipers that crawled among the rocks, of robbers who attacked from behind the barren hills?

Standing close to the wall, she strained to hear what the men were saying, but their voices were too low.

Abital opened the door and stepped into the room. "That young man is here."

"Yes, I know."

"You'll be pleasant to him, won't you?"

Huldah gave a mirthless laugh. "He's not here on a social visit to me. He's discussing something with Father."

"But," her mother insisted, "if you have a chance to speak with . . ." A sharp knock at the door and Barak's hearty voice interrupted her. "Daughter, come to my room."

Huldah smoothed her hair and quickly draped a shawl over her head. At the door to his room, her father took her by the arm. "Shallum is waiting for you."

As she entered the room, he stepped toward her and reached for her hand. His touch sent a quiver through her, and her hand trembled in his. Looking up at him, she noticed an eager light shining in his eyes.

"The . . . the princess?" she stammered.

"Miriama reported to me that all is well with Jedidah and her two sons."

"I am grateful." She took a deep breath and asked, "What does she want me to do?"

"Nothing this time," he answered laughing.

Barak cleared his throat. "I have given this young man the privilege of telling you what he and I have discussed."

Shallum dropped her hand and straightened his shoulders. "Because my mission in Jerusalem has certain disadvantages, I have hesitated to declare my intention." Looking intently into her eyes, he stopped speaking.

Huldah frowned in puzzlement. His intention! Could he mean . . . ? No, he couldn't mean his intention for her.

"The time had come to speak to your father. You are the woman I want."

She was silent, unable to absorb the impact of his words . . . words she couldn't believe were true.

"Your father and I agree that you shall become my wife."

"Oh!" she gasped. "I thought you would want to marry

a woman of noble birth. I thought you and Miriama . . ." In confusion she glanced around the room.

Shallum shook his head. "No, not her. You are the woman I want. Let me tell you," he entreated gently. "When Josiah was born, Jedidah's father commissioned me to leave southern Judah, to watch over his grandson in Jerusalem. Of course, I'm not allowed to visit the princess in her chambers, so she appointed Miriama to carry messages." He drew Huldah to him, and then his arms were around her. "Only the princess knows that Miriama is my sister."

"Your sister! That's why she asked me what I thought of you." As she lifted her face to his, her shawl fell to the floor. At that moment she remembered that her father was still in the room. Turning her head, she saw his solid figure in the doorway, silhouetted against the glow of the torches. The rain had ceased, and he was gazing into the sky.

Shallum's eager lips on hers sent a shiver of excitement through her body. "Tomorrow I'll arrange with your father for the betrothal ceremony," he whispered. Slowly he released her from his embrace and then entered the courtyard to take leave of her father.

After he went out the gate and when Abital and Kezia finally ended their excited chatter about the betrothal feast, Huldah lay on her bed, pondering what had happened to her this evening. With a prayer of thanksgiving on her lips, she fell asleep.

The next evening Shallum arrived to discuss the betrothal arrangements with her father. They set the date for seven days later and agreed that Barak would provide a witness. While her father stood near the door to his room, Shallum lingered in the courtyard with his arm around Huldah's waist and his head close to hers. She listened to his whisper of love and raised her face for his kiss.

The day of the betrothal Abital and Kezia bustled around the kitchen, preparing barley and onion soup, roasted turtledoves, wheat bread, and raisin cakes. "If only he had declared himself last summer instead of in the spring, we could have served apricots and pomegranates," Kezia complained.

"Hush!" ordered Abital. "We're glad it happened any time of the year."

While they fussed about the food, Huldah retreated to her room. Already she knew she wanted to wear the blue linen. Now she removed it from the chest and lovingly smoothed its folds. She would always treasure this blue robe. Whenever she looked at the fabric, she thought of the first time she had considered buying it—that day she saw the man in the brown robe watching her from a shoemaker's shop. How irritated she had felt! And now he was the man she loved. Hugging the blue linen to her breast, she breathed in deep contentment.

While she dabbed fragrant lily of the valley perfume on her temples and wrists, she wondered if her father would insist on the usual one-year betrothal before the marriage ceremony. Such a long time to wait!

But still, a familiar worry returned; her father was betrothing her to a man of noble birth. Was she capable of living up to the duties of a nobleman's wife? Entertaining rich guests? Dressing in fine gowns and wearing expensive jewelry?

Dressed and ready long before Shallum and the witness were due to arrive, Huldah reached to the hidden shelf for a scroll. In the quietness of her room, she read, "O give thanks to the Lord for He is good. . . . Let the redeemed of the Lord say so." Her thoughts raced back to the night she carried Josiah to the Temple. Today in her joy and excitement about the betrothal she had forgotten to pray for the boy's safety. The reality of danger for the small prince returned to assail her, and she offered a fervent petition to God. "Lord, watch over him. Protect him."

Out in the courtyard, Barak paced back and forth in the sunshine as he waited for his guests. The scribe appeared first. He was of Barak's age but fat and slow moving. Soon afterward the call came, "Open for Shallum, son of Tikvah." Huldah's heart leaped, and hastily she replaced the scroll on its shelf. Old Samuel opened the gate.

She heard her father's greeting of welcome and Shallum's reply. Then their voices grew indistinct as Barak led the men into the dining area. Huldah stepped into the kitchen. "Mother, do you want me to serve the soup?"

Flushed from working over the fire, Abital wiped her face with a cloth. "Your father decided that you will sit at the table."

"I've never eaten with his guests before." Huldah's words protested, but her heart beat in happy anticipation.

"Your father has spoken. He says for this special occasion you will eat with them, but first he and the young man must come to some agreements."

Huldah withdrew to a bench at the far side of the courtyard. A shaft of late afternoon sunlight slanted across the top of the wall and touched her cheek. A slight breeze brought the warm smell of roasting turtledoves. She heard her mother in the kitchen stirring the barley soup, and Kezia taking bowls from a shelf.

Conversation from the dining room was low and guarded. At last her father emerged. She stood up and walked hesitantly toward him. "We have completed the betrothal contract," he assured her. "Shallum has offered a sufficient dowry for you. Also he will purchase a house and arrange for necessary servants."

"Thank you, Father."

"For my part I will provide your apparel and a marriage feast fit for a nobleman and his bride." He lowered his voice. "I have also agreed to an early wedding date—six months from now instead of the usual one year. Shallum says he has delayed long enough, and I think it's best to have you married before you're too old."

Six months instead of a year! She let out an elated cry. "This pleases you," declared Barak with amusement.

"Yes."

"Then let us celebrate." He shouted toward the kitchen, "Kezia . . . serve the dinner." Taking hold of his daughter's arm, he escorted her to the dining room. "Now go in and pay your respect to your future husband and the witness."

She took a deep breath and stepped into the room. Shallum reached for her hand and led her to the chair next to his. With him so close, she forgot for a moment the words she had practiced. Regaining her composure she managed to say, "Father, I'm grateful to you for arranging this betrothal."

Carrying a large pot of steaming soup, Kezia shuffled into the room. Abital followed with a platter of roasted doves. Then they brought loaves of wheat bread, raisin cakes, and jugs of wine. Bustling around the table, the two women served the men and Huldah. During the long, unhurried meal, she remained silent. Whenever Shallum looked her way and his lips curved into a smile, her heart sang.

At last Barak stood up. He faced Shallum and delivered the traditional words, "You shall be my son-in-law."

The younger man rose and, taking Huldah's hand, assisted her to her feet. From beneath his leather waistband, he drew a golden necklace and placed it around her neck. "See by this token you are set apart for me, according to the law of Moses."

With quavering voice she replied, "I accept your token." She heard her mother's joyful cry, and then the men's exuberant shouts filled the room.

The following morning Abital hurried into Huldah's room. "We must go to the wool merchant's shop for your wedding fabric."

"Yes," agreed the bride-to-be, "I want to start the embroidery right away."

At that moment Shallum's call came from the street. Huldah glanced down at the plain robe she was wearing. "I didn't expect him today. He said nothing about taking me to the princess this morning." When he entered the courtyard and she saw the pained expression on his face, she hurried to him. "What is it?"

"Josiah is safe," he answered as he took both her hands in his. "But when Prince Amon found out that I had planned our marriage, he decreed that no one from the palace shall marry until his father returns from captivity."

She clung to him and choked out, "That could mean years . . . or never."

He held her close, and she could feel his labored breathing. "We can't give up hope," he said. Slowly he released her. "Meanwhile, the princess has requested your presence. Tomorrow I'll return to accompany you to the palace so you can teach the ladies of the court." He turned away and motioned for Samuel to open the gate.

When he was gone, Huldah raised her head and pleaded, "Help me, O Lord. Give me comfort and strength."

The next morning Shallum arrived with a water pouch slung over his shoulder. "Some days I go outside the city wall and offer water to travelers. If you would accompany me, we could have more time together."

She nodded happily. "I'll go with you."

She followed him out a city gate and down into the Kidron Valley on the east side of the Temple mount. They climbed a short way up another mount and sat under one of the olive trees. "We'll wait here," he said.

"It's so peaceful," Huldah remarked, "and a good place to look toward the Temple."

"Whenever I'm here," replied Shallum, "I pray that God will remember the people of Judah, that we will not always suffer. I pray also that before too long you and I can marry." He reached for the water pouch. "Some travelers are approaching."

She watched him walk down the hill and raise his hand in the salutation of peace. Here on the quiet hillside away from the city's turmoil, she could try to forget some of the disappointments and worries that plagued her. At her feet tiny white daisies blossomed, and a snail made its slow way through the grass.

Huldah watched while five men drank from Shallum's water pouch. Appearing satisfied with his task, he returned to escort her to the palace. When she entered Jedidah's chambers, Josiah ran to meet her. She swooped him into her arms as he laughed and tried to say her name.

The little boy's mother smiled. "Your name is one of his first words." She held a baby. "Come and see my second son." With Josiah still in her arms, Huldah stood beside the princess to admire the dark-haired infant.

Daily Huldah accompanied Shallum outside the city wall and sat under a tree while he offered water to thirsty travelers. Spring gave way to the heat of summer, summer to autumn. One morning she hiked with him to the top of the mount where they gazed over the hills of Judah. He put his arms around her and held her while she sobbed out her frustration over their lost wedding plans.

During the cool winter months, Shallum took Huldah directly to the palace, but when spring showed its first warm day, he invited her again to the Kidron Valley. While she waited under an olive tree, she noticed a flurry of migrating turtledoves flying north, and she thought of her betrothal dinner. Already a year had passed, and still she remained unmarried.

Before long Shallum returned from serving water to three men. When he sat down next to her, she wondered at the sad expression on his face. After some moments of silence he said, "These men have traveled all the way from Babylon. They bring news that the king of Assyria has agreed to release King Manasseh."

"Then at last we can marry!" she exclaimed in delight, but when she looked at him, he was frowning. Suddenly he held his hands to his head and a deep groan escaped from his throat.

Chapter 6

Huldah placed her hand on his arm and waited. Without looking at her, Shallum spoke in a hushed voice, "Prince Amon has promised that if ever his father returns from captivity, he will honor him with a great festival." He paused, once again groaning. "Amon says that during the celebration he will burn his firstborn son—the most valuable gift possible—in the fires of Molech in gratitude for his father's safe return."

Huldah cried out, "Not my baby, not Josiah!"

"You have to remember that Josiah is not yours," he admonished her gently. "He belongs to Amon."

She stood up and scanned the valley. "Where are the travelers? You must stop them from telling the prince about his father's release."

"It's too late. They're already on their way to the royal court. They expect to claim a reward for bringing the news."

Kneeling next to Shallum, she grasped his arm. "Amon

mustn't sacrifice Josiah. What can we do to save him from the fires of Molech?"

Slowly he answered, "I have spent many sleepless nights considering what to do. There's a priest, a Benjaminite, in the town of Anathoth. He comes once a year to take his turn offering sacrifices in the Temple, and he offers only to God not to idols. We have become friends."

"Can you take Josiah to him?"

"I'll try, and if it is too risky to stay there, I'll journey east to the other side of the Jordan River."

"Is it safe to go there?"

"Any place is safer for Josiah than here in Jerusalem!"

Huldah bent her head to his shoulder, "It's so dangerous. What if . . . ?"

"Let's not think of what might go wrong." With his arm around her, he stood up. "Now I must take you to the princess."

"Yes, of course," she answered, but after hearing of Amon's plan, how could she concentrate on teaching? They walked in silence to the palace. When Huldah entered Jedidah's chambers, the princess was holding Josiah and singing to him. She stopped in the middle of her happy song. "What's the matter?"

She hasn't heard, Huldah realized. *If Shallum knows about Amon's plan, surely others do also. But no court lady or servant has been brave enough to inform Jedidah that her husband will sacrifice their son. Someone must tell her.* She took a deep breath. "I have just learned distressing news."

"Your father—or mother?"

Josiah wandered across the room to Huldah, and she picked him up. "My parents are in good health. The news concerns . . ."

A shout outside the door broke into her speech. The door crashed open, and Prince Amon marched in. "The

51

Assyrians have released my father, and he's on his way to Jerusalem. He grabbed Josiah from Huldah, and the boy started to cry. "My father will know that I welcome him home when I sacrifice my firstborn son to Molech." He swung the screaming child violently around and dropped him onto a couch. "Keep him safe and in good health until my father comes," he admonished Jedidah. "I want a body without blemish to sacrifice. I must offer my very best." He left as abruptly as he had entered. Still yelling in fright, Josiah sat on the couch and stared at the door through which his father had disappeared.

Jedidah stood completely still—rigid and white-faced. Huldah rushed to her and led her to the couch. "Sit here."

Wailing and sobbing, the princess cried out, "No, no, no! He mustn't do that to Josiah." She put one arm around her son and pressed his head against her breast.

Huldah leaned down and whispered, "Shallum knows, and he has a plan."

"A plan? What plan?"

"He can take Josiah to someone he trusts in a town north of Jerusalem."

Jedidah lifted the sleeve of her tunic to wipe away her tears. "Yes, he must take him. Tell Shallum to take him tonight, otherwise it might be too late. When you go to teach your class, ask Miriama to come here. I need her help."

Huldah reached out to pat Josiah's back, and then reluctantly left the room.

After delivering the message to Miriama, she toiled through the lesson with the ladies of the court. At the same time her mind raced ahead to the unknown consequences of Shallum's plan. Could he smuggle the little boy out of the palace and slip past numerous guards? Could he outdistance pursuers all the way to Anathoth or the eastern lands? Would she ever again see the child she loved . . . or the man she wanted to marry?

A subdued Miriama led her to the gate where Shallum waited. On the way to her father's house, he did not speak, but after they entered the courtyard, he pulled her into his arms. Holding her to him, with his head touching hers, he whispered, "I'll take Josiah tonight."

For a long moment Huldah clung to him before she could let him go. After the gate closed behind him, she listened to his fading footsteps. To avoid the chatter of her mother and Kezia in the kitchen, she retreated to the quietness of her room.

Sometime during the night a loud knocking awakened her. She heard her father walk across the courtyard and speak to the watchmen he had hired to guard his gate. "What's the matter out there?"

"There's a woman here who says she has a message for you."

"At this time of night?"

"Please, let me in," the woman pleaded.

Recognizing Miriama's voice, Huldah left her room and ran to her father. "It's Shallum's sister."

He unbarred the gate. As soon as Miriama hurried in, Huldah put her arm around the young woman's trembling shoulders.

"What's this all about?" Barak demanded.

Between deep sobs, words came. "The plan failed. Guards caught Shallum with Josiah. They've taken my brother to the dungeon, and Amon grabbed his son and has hidden him somewhere in the palace. Jedidah doesn't know where."

"Oh, no!" cried Huldah.

"Speak quietly, you two," ordered Barak. "This is threatening information."

"You are right, my lord," replied Miriama politely. "It's dangerous for me to relate this information and for you to hear it. But I must tell you more. Prince Amon says that if Huldah returns to the palace or even walks in the city streets, he will have his soldiers arrest her and . . ."

"And?" prompted Barak.

". . . and execute her."

"Stupid, incompetent fool," growled Huldah's father. "When will we ever have an end to all these depraved times in Judah?"

Miriama adjusted her shawl to cover most of her face. "I must hurry back to the princess."

Huldah hugged her. "How will you get into the palace again?"

"I know a way. There's a captain of the guard who will help me."

"Go then," said Barak, "and may God go with you." The remainder of that night Huldah lay awake. Too many questions pressed down upon her. Would Amon order his soldiers to take Shallum out to the Hinnom Valley and strike him down? Or would the prince throw him in a damp dungeon and leave him without enough food and water until he wasted away? Or was Amon perhaps planning an elaborate execution as part of Manasseh's homecoming celebration? And where was Josiah? She pictured the two-year-old boy, locked in a box, frightened, and crying for his mother. *And I can't even go to the princess to sympathize with her*, thought Huldah. *I'm a prisoner in my father's house.*

The days passed slowly. Each morning she walked in the courtyard. Coriander growing in pots showed its lacy white blossoms. Thyme produced a display of tiny lavender flowers. In the kitchen she shaped bread dough into loaves. In her room she tried to concentrate on reading. She spoke little to her parents and Kezia, and they in turn

54

respected her grief over Shallum and Josiah.

Autumn arrived, then winter. Every day old Samuel ventured out to the marketplace, where he listened for news and gossip. Although travelers arrived from the north, they carried no reports about when the king of Assyria would release Manasseh. Then one morning when Samuel returned from his daily trip, he was hardly inside the courtyard wall before he announced, "Big excitement. Our king and a remnant of the men captured with him are a two-day's journey from Jerusalem."

Huldah ran to her room and threw herself onto the bed. The time for Amon's big celebration had come. Now he would offer Josiah as a burnt offering to Molech. Now . . . Shallum. Sobs ripped from her throat.

Two days later many of the citizens waited in the streets for the return of their king—not out of love but out of curiosity. Amon, dressed in his most elaborate robe and jewelry, marched out with an honor guard of a thousand men to meet his father.

That afternoon Huldah was surprised to see Barak come home early. He seated himself on a bench in the courtyard and shook his head. "It's hard to believe. I hope it's true."

She stood in front of him. "What's hard to believe?"

"I was there and heard it myself. King Manasseh entered the city and climbed up a stairway onto the city wall. There he proclaimed in a loud voice that when he was in prison, he repented of his sinful ways and asked the Lord to render his enemies merciful. In answer to his prayers, the Assyrians released him, and God brought him to Jerusalem. In return Manasseh will worship only the one true God. He will allow no sacrifices to Baal or Molech or any other foreign idol."

"That means Josiah is safe!" exclaimed Huldah. "But do

you think the king will release Shallum?"

"We must not give up hope."

All the next day she listened to footsteps in the street, but none were the ones she wanted to hear. The second morning a winter rain blew in from the west. She huddled by her hearth, shelling dried red lentils for barley and lentil porridge. Raindrops pounded onto the courtyard stones, drowning out any sound from the street. When Samuel's cracking voice announced, "A guest is here," Huldah raised her head in surprise. Shallum stood inside the gate, water running off his heavy woolen cloak.

She ran to him and pulled him to the warmth of the kitchen hearth. "Let me hang up your cloak by the fire." He removed it, and she hung it onto wooden pegs that projected from the wall.

When she turned around, Shallum held out his hands to her, "Josiah is with his mother again."

"Thanks to God," said Huldah. His hands were cold in her warm ones, and his cheek felt cool against hers. When she put her arms around him, she could feel the thinness of his body through his robe and tunic. "You lost weight while you were in that dungeon."

"Some days I had only a handful of parched wheat to eat, other days a small loaf of barley bread."

"I've been so worried about you and waited so long to see you."

"Yesterday I had business to attend to."

Of *course*, she thought as she drew herself out of his embrace, *he has more important business than coming to see me. I must always remember that he is a nobleman working for the king.*

Chapter 7

Yesterday," he continued, "I bought a house." So that was his business—a house. Huldah clasped her hands together in delight. "Does that mean we can set a new date for our wedding?"

He grinned at her. "After I leave here I'll go to the scribes' quarters to talk to your father about the marriage feast."

The exciting thought sent a fluttering to her heart. Smiling, she asked, "Where is the house?"

"In the second quarter, the new section that King Hezekiah built shortly before he died."

"Near the Temple mount?"

"Yes. And I've also hired the servants—two cooks and three maidservants for you, two menservants for me, and, of course, a doorkeeper for inside and guards for outside the gate."

Huldah's smile faded. "Do we need so many?" He cupped her face in his hands. "I want you to have all the help you need. The house has numerous rooms and a large banquet hall. King Manasseh has promoted me to become chief keeper of his wardrobe, and with this new position, I'll need to entertain guests in our home." His gentle kiss gave her hope that she could live up to his expectations. He took his cloak from the wall. "I'll go now to see your father."

The smell of warm wool from his cloak lingered in the kitchen. Huldah stared into the fire . . . chief keeper of the king's wardrobe . . . a large house, many servants, a banquet room for important guests . . . the duties of a nobleman's wife.

* * *

King Manasseh lost no time in implementing his reforms. He ordered his servants to take all the images and altars of idols from the Temple mount and throw them into the Hinnom Valley. He hired workers to strengthen the city's fortifications, to repair the walls, build towers, and construct an outer wall around the west and north sides of Jerusalem. In the Temple the priests restored the Lord's altar and offered sacrifices of peace and thanksgiving. "In all of Judah," Manasseh commanded, "we will serve only the one true God."

* * *

"Your father has agreed to a marriage feast at the second new moon," Shallum announced to Huldah. "This will give me time to prepare our home."

"And for my preparations . . ." she answered with thoughts racing ahead to packing clothes and her most priceless possessions—her scrolls.

Abital and Kezia plunged into activity—plans for the

feast, shopping for supplies. Along with Barak and the bride-to-be they accepted Shallum's invitation to inspect his house. Surveying the banquet room, Abital nodded her approval. "Nice and big. Just the right size for a wedding feast."

Kezia added her opinions. "The kitchen is large enough to roast the lambs."

After wandering in and out of the rooms, Huldah stood with Shallum in the courtyard. "I didn't realize the house was so large, and it even has its own cistern."

He squeezed her hand. "I wanted to give you a pleasant surprise."

On the wedding day, Miriama appeared at Barak's house to help dress the bride. In Huldah's room, the two young women gazed at each other. "You probably have wondered why I talked so much about Shallum," Miriama said. "From the first time I saw you, I felt you were the woman for him."

Huldah touched Miriama's hand. "Thank you. I've never had a sister. Now I have you."

"And I have you." She laughed happily. "May I help prepare my new sister for the wedding feast?"

In their newfound friendship, Miriama confided that she was in love with Enosh, a captain of the king's guard, and Huldah confessed her concern about marrying into a family of noble birth.

"You may not have been born into such a family, but I think you're truly as noble as my brother or I." She glanced around the room. "Now where's your wedding gown?"

Huldah removed it from an acacia-wood chest. Miriama unfolded the clean, white goat's wool set off with elaborate blue, yellow, and red embroidery. "It's lovely."

Stroking the soft fabric, the bride added, "I've waited a long time to wear it."

Later in the day Miriama opened a box. "I brought my strings of pearls and turquoise to adorn your hair. We want you to look like a queen." Along with the jewels, she fashioned Huldah's brown hair into thick braids. She placed the golden betrothal necklace around the bride's neck and draped the embroidered woolen shawl over her head.

At dusk all preparations were complete. Abital and Kezia returned from Shallum's house where they had supervised the roasting of lambs for the feast. Dressed in fine robes, the family waited for the groom to arrive. Even the doorkeeper Samuel wore a new cloak.

"For lo, the winter is past, the rain is over and gone," Huldah quoted from one of her scrolls. "The flowers appear on the earth, the time of singing has come, and the voice of the turtledove is heard in our land."

"That's beautiful," sighed Miriama.

"The turtledoves remind me of the night that Shallum and I carried Josiah to the Temple mount. I wish I could see that little boy at my wedding."

"It cannot happen. Prince Amon has refused to allow the princess to attend, but the ladies of the court will come."

At the sound of singing in the street, Miriama fastened a veil over Huldah's face. Shallum's voice rang out, "Open for Shallum, son of Tikvah. I have come for my bride, Huldah, daughter of Barak."

Samuel had the honor of opening the gate for the groom and the group of men with him. Huldah's father led her to him and placed her hand in his. Barak removed the veil that covered his daughter's face and placed the veil on Shallum's shoulder. Then he declared the traditional words, "The government of his household shall be upon his shoulder." The guests shouted their approval, drowning out the sounds of Abital's and Kezia's joyful sobs.

Huldah held tightly to Shallum's arm, needing support for the excitement that caused her knees to feel weak. Without her veil, she could see that he was dressed as a king. He had gained weight, and the ornate robe fit well. On his head he wore a golden crown, and in his hand he carried another. When he placed it on Huldah's head, the guests renewed their shouting.

Barak's voice carried above the boisterous congratulations. "Let the procession begin." As he strode out the gate, the bridal couple followed behind him, and the guests trailed along. Abital, Kezia, and Miriama walked together. Each person carried a small clay lamp with a single wick burning in olive oil. The men sang a lively melody, and from somewhere in the street ahead, women's voices joined the song. As the procession turned down a side street, Huldah saw the ladies of the court. Light from their lamps illuminated the passageway.

In the banquet room of the new house, Huldah and Shallum sat under a canopy of green cypress boughs and fragrant spring flowers. During the leisurely meal, Huldah took her place as queen of the feast and, along with Shallum, responded regally to the guests' benedictions and her father's blessing: "May you increase to thousands upon thousands; may your offspring possess the gates of their enemies."

Late in the night the ladies of the court ushered the bride to a richly decorated bedchamber. Soon the groom's friends brought him. Alone together in the room, Shallum slowly lifted the crown from his head and gave it to Huldah. In turn she removed hers and handed it to him. They placed their crowns side by side on a table, and she stepped closer to him. His arms encircled her, and her heart sang, *I'm married to the man I love.*

* * *

The feasting continued for seven days, and then Huldah became mistress of her household, learning to deal with the servants and the large number of rooms. At the proper time, 30 days after the wedding, she returned to the palace. No longer needing an escort now that she was married, she walked alone through the streets. When she entered the women's garden, she heard a squeal of laughter. Josiah raced down a path and into her arms. The Egyptian dog joined in, leaping and barking a welcome. Huldah hugged the little boy and patted the hound. Miriama greeted her, "The princess is waiting for you." They left Josiah under the watchful care of three maidservants.

Before they entered Jedidah's chambers, a Nubian slave addressed Huldah. "King Manasseh knows that you are here and he requests your presence."

"Me?" She grabbed Miriama's hand. "Why would he want to see me?"

Miriama's eyes were wide with alarm. "I don't know, but you'll have to do as he orders."

Reluctantly Huldah let go of her sister-in-law's hand. Taking a deep breath, she followed the slave through a long passageway to a heavy door. The door opened and two soldiers ushered her into a wider hall and down stone steps to the royal buildings where the monarch conducted business. Shivering from the unheated corridors and deep apprehension, Huldah waited while the soldiers announced her arrival. She heard the king's voice. "Let the woman enter."

Expecting to see a dazzling room with ornate tapestries and ivory throne, she stared in surprise at the small chamber. The king, dressed in a plain white robe, stood near a window. "Are you Huldah, wife of Shallum, the keeper of my wardrobe?"

"Yes, my lord."

"Do you teach the ladies of the court to read?"

Will he condemn me to a dungeon for teaching without his permission?

Faintly she answered, "Yes, my lord."

"From now on I want you to enlarge your school to include the wives and daughters of my captains and city officials."

Huldah blinked in relief, and a great joy surged through her. She could teach even more women to read.

Manasseh motioned to a window that opened to the south. "Come over here." In a confusion of awe she stepped to the window, where the king pointed down to the wall of the building.

"See those gates that lead into the royal court and the palace? I will send out a proclamation that certain women shall attend your school, and I will instruct my guards to allow them through those gates." He turned away from the window, "From now on you will no longer use Sumerian writings. You will teach the history of our people, using scrolls that I keep in my library."

"Thank you, my lord."

In the passageways, Huldah walked with her head up and a smile on her lips. *My school! I can teach from Hebrew scrolls—the prophecies of Isaiah and history from our chronicles.*

* * *

In the months that followed, Huldah greeted each day in happy anticipation of satisfying hours with her students. The school flourished. Women from the city came to learn, and the court ladies continued their studies.

With Manasseh's reforms and the hiring of workmen to repair the city's old walls and build new ones, prosperity returned to Jerusalem. Trade with other countries increased, benefiting all of Judah. Priests in the Temple sacrificed only to the one true God.

In an appropriate celebration, Miriama married Enosh, the captain of the guards, and during the next two years she produced a daughter and then a son.

But for Huldah and Shallum no babies arrived. "My happiness would be complete," she told her husband, "If I could give you a son."

In the cool of a summer evening, they were sitting on the roof of their home. From here they could see the dark outline of Solomon's Temple against light that lingered in the sky. A meaty smell of smoke from the last of the day's sacrifices drifted in the still air.

"I, too, long for a son," Shallum answered, "but if God chooses not to send one, we must accept His judgment." After a moment he added, "Often I think of Josiah as our son. The princess is generous to share him with us."

"Yes, she is, and she's told me that Prince Amon doesn't know how close we are to his son."

"It's safer if he doesn't know." Shallum shook his head. "It seems only a short time ago that we took Josiah to the priest for redemption, and now he's already five years old. The court scribe says Josiah reads well for his age."

"Yes, sometimes he reads to me. He's a bright child. That's just as well since he'll soon become king."

Shallum shifted on his chair and leaned toward her. "What makes you think he will soon become king?"

"I don't know. It's just a feeling I have."

He laid his hand on her arm. "You've mentioned other events before they happened. Do you think God's given you a gift? Might He have given you the ability to prophesy?"

"Oh! I don't think so." Huldah shrank back against her chair. "If that was true, what would the Lord expect of me?"

Chapter 8

He would expect you to interpret his messages for the people."

"But most prophets are men," Huldah protested.

Shallum's voice was gentle, yet firm. "Not all. Don't forget Deborah—and Moses' sister, Miriama. If God has chosen you to receive His gift of interpreting messages, you must accept it."

She gazed down at the rooftop and shook her head, "I'm not good enough."

"No one's good enough. Even Moses' sister displeased the Lord for awhile, but he forgave her."

Reaching for the comfort of her husband's hand, she fretted, "I wouldn't know how to begin."

"You've always trusted in the Lord. I'm sure He'll tell you what to do."

"I have trusted, but He's never asked me to do something so hard."

As the days passed, the idea that she possessed the

gift of prophecy seldom left Huldah's mind. *Has the Lord really chosen me to serve in this way?* she wondered. *If so, am I capable of using His gift to interpret messages? When would He expect me to begin?*

One morning while Huldah was teaching the ladies, a maidservant timidly entered the room.

"Why are you here?" Miriama asked.

"King Manasseh has sent a message," the woman answered. "He requests the presence of the teacher."

A shiver passed through Huldah. *Why has the king called me again? Have I displeased him in some way?* She followed the servant out of the room and down the long halls and passageways to the royal courts. This time the king waited for her in his ornate reception room. Golden tapestries covered the walls, and he sat on an ivory throne. Numerous courtiers stood behind and to the sides of him. Court scribes sat at tables. Before Huldah bowed her head to the king, she caught a glimpse of her husband standing among the men.

"Huldah, wife of Shallum," Manasseh greeted her, "I have made a decision about you."

She clasped her hands together to control their trembling. "Yes, my lord."

"I know that you have studied our history and the writings of our prophets. Men as well as women could benefit from your counsel. Therefore I ordered workmen to prepare a room for you in the marketplace at the city center. It is now ready, and you will sit there three days of each week to receive any person who wishes to inquire about messages from God."

"Yes, my lord," Huldah gasped her polite response, but without thinking more words tumbled out, "You want me to interpret God's messages?"

"Wait!" Prince Amon pushed his way through the

courtiers and stood between his father and Huldah. "No woman should sit in the center of the city and act like some sort of prophet. It's not right for any woman, especially this one who is married to that traitor Shallum."

The king stood up. "I have spoken, and I repeat that this woman will sit in the center of the city and receive any person who wishes to inquire about God's messages. Her presence there will show the people that I believe in the Lord's guidance." He looked directly at his son. "My soldiers will guard her." Turning to Huldah he said, "I dismiss you to your duties."

Agonizing over Amon's hostility to Shallum, she backed out of the room and into the passageway. As she hurried toward the women's quarters, familiar footsteps sounded behind her. Stopping at a window that overlooked a garden, she waited for her husband. "I'll have soldiers to guard me," she blurted, "but you won't have them to protect you from Prince Amon."

"As long as King Manasseh is alive," he assured her, "I have nothing to worry about."

She pressed her face against his shoulder but could not speak.

The next morning Huldah got up early to choose which scroll to carry with her to the marketplace. Spreading several on her table, she considered them carefully. *In case I need to find answers in a prophet's writings*, she decided, I'll take Isaiah's.

Before Shallum left for his work at the palace, he held her in his steady embrace. "With the Lord's help, you'll do well."

"Without His help, I could never interpret His messages."

When two soldiers arrived to escort her to the city center, she was ready. One soldier walked in front and one followed as they paraded her through the familiar streets. Shoppers on their way to market paused to stare at Huldah and her escorts.

With a start she realized the soldiers were heading away from the marketplace. She hurried to catch up with the guard in front of her. "Where are you taking me?"

"To the scribes' quarters."

"Why?"

"King Manasseh's orders. He wants the scribes to see you on your way to the marketplace."

To the scribes' quarters! Although she had sent a message to her parents telling them about her assignment, what would her father think if the soldiers paraded her through his place of business?

The street entered the scribes' quarters through an archway and ran the length of the long building. On both sides of the indoor street, scribes sat on platforms. Low, wooden walls divided the platforms into stalls for each man's designated place. Large windows and unroofed sections of the building let in sufficient light for the scribes to see while using their writing reeds and ink on papyrus.

Clients were already arriving to seek help in conducting the day's business, and a confusion of voices echoed throughout the working place.

Probably the people here think the soldiers have arrested me, Huldah fretted, *and are marching me around the city as a bad example before taking me to prison.*

Some men frowned at her, others shook their heads. Her father's place lay at the far end. She saw him standing near his table, and when close enough, she was relieved to see him smiling at her. All too quickly the soldiers hurried her past.

Out of the building, she soon heard the usual sounds from the marketplace where vendors called out their wares to shoppers. Their voices grew louder as the soldiers guided her through a narrow street to the market's open section. Here the sides of the street broadened to form a wide area where vendors sold food, and peddlers spread their goods on the stones. At one side, walls of a new mud-brick booth supported a wooden roof. The lead soldier pointed to the booth. "This is the place the king ordered for you." Leaving her there, the guards wandered across the market area to a seller of almonds and dates.

Through the booth's open front, Huldah saw a small table and two benches. She stepped up to the stone floor and placed the scroll on the table. What if no one came? Would anyone want to inquire of a woman prophet? Unrolling the papyrus, she sat down to read from the words of Isaiah. "Trust in the Lord forever, for the Lord God is an everlasting Rock."

Looking up from her reading, she saw two little boys in ragged robes standing by her step. "What are you going to sell?" the smaller boy asked.

She found the boys and their eager question appealing. "I'm not going to sell anything. King Manasseh said that I would sit here to answer questions anyone has about God's messages."

"Has anyone asked a question?"

"Not yet."

The older boy's face brightened. "We'll go find someone for you." And they dashed away.

Huldah smiled at their exuberance but doubted they would find someone to bring.

Across the way the soldiers were munching on dates and almonds while they chatted with an attractive young woman. Near them a baker checked the fire in his large oven. Huldah could see round loaves of unbaked bread on a table inside the man's stall. Next to him a grain merchant was measuring wheat and pouring it into a tightly-woven basket for a servant woman. A donkey loaded with leather passed the stalls, and its driver directed the animal toward the sandalmakers' street.

On one side of Huldah's booth, a spice merchant's shop gave forth the aroma of sweet basil and spicy cinnamon. On the other side, a fruit vendor called to passing shoppers, "Pomegranates. Ripe, red pomegranates, ready to eat."

A man approached Huldah's stall. "Father!" she exclaimed in happy surprise.

A proud expression crossed his face. "Just now the crier of daily news passed through the scribes' quarters and announced that the prophetess Huldah was seated in the marketplace. I have come to welcome you to the center of the city."

"Thank you, Father, but do you think anyone will come to ask for my counsel?"

He glanced behind him. "I see two little boys directing a man this way."

She bit her lip and wiped her perspiring hands on the sleeves of her robe. "I'm ready."

The man stepped up and seated himself on the opposite bench. "The crier of daily news said that a prophetess in the marketplace could answer questions about the worship of God. I have come for some answers."

Huldah took a deep breath and silently prayed, *Help me, Lord.*

* * *

Before long, she settled into a routine of counseling those who asked about God's messages, teaching the women, and reading with Josiah. She and Shallum lived comfortably in their home, only now and then mentioning the apprehension that lay close to the surface in their thoughts—dread of the time when Amon might begin his reign.

It was on a hazy autumn day that King Manasseh suddenly became ill. By the next morning he was dead. Cries and wailing filled the streets as the period of lamentation began for the king.

That day the soldiers did not arrive to escort Huldah to her place in the city center.

"I have to go to the palace and choose the proper robe for the king's burial," Shallum told her.

"No, you mustn't. It's not safe for you."

"It may not be safe, but it's still my duty." After he left, Huldah wandered from room to room, trying to stay out of the way of the maidservants, who were scrubbing the floors and sweeping the courtyard. She was in the kitchen conferring with the cooks when she heard a call at the gate.

When the doorkeeper opened for her, Miriama stumbled into the courtyard and dropped onto a bench. "It's happened again," she sobbed. "They've taken Shallum to the dungeon."

Huldah held her hands over her face and sank onto the bench next to her sister-in-law. "Oh, no. He shouldn't have gone to the palace this morning."

Miriama put her arm around Huldah's shoulders. "They would have come here to get him."

"What will they do to him?"

"I don't know, but Enosh says that when he's on duty, he'll make sure none of his guards mistreat Shallum. He also told me to advise you to remain inside your house. You're safer here." Quickly she hugged Huldah and then stood up. "I'm sorry I can't stay longer."

"You'll come whenever there's news, won't you?"

"Whenever I can."

Alone again in the courtyard Huldah sat on the bench in stunned silence. *In prison, in prison, my husband is in prison*, echoed through her mind. "How long, Lord," she begged to know, "How long can we expect our new king to give these cruel orders?"

His father had reigned for 55 years. But in a shorter time Amon could bring about more corruption than Manasseh had before the Assyrians captured him.

To the citizens of Jerusalem, Amon announced, "My father was a strong man before he went into captivity. I will rule as he did at that time. I will provide altars for Baal and set up asherim—the wooden pillars for Asherah, goddess of fertility." Soon workmen retrieved the idols that Manasseh had thrown into the Hinnom Valley. They hauled them to the mount and set them in the courtyard and in the Temple.

Once again a prisoner in her house, Huldah fought against the deep worry that threatened to overwhelm her. She longed to see her husband, to hear his footsteps arriving home, to feel his arms around her. Without enough food, was he growing thin and weaker each day? She wished she could carry provisions to him—almonds, dried apricots, a loaf of wheat bread.

Miriama brought news. "Whenever he can, Enosh smuggles extra food to Shallum."

Huldah squeezed her sister-in-law's hand. "Tell your husband that I'm grateful."

A note of despair crept into Miriama's voice. "King Amon pays tribute to the Assyrians, and he's doing all in his power to please them. He has ordered worship of all the pagan idols, not just Baal and Asherah."

"Even . . . even Molech?"

"Even Molech. Some of the courtiers are against

Amon's concessions to the Assyrians and worship of idols, but they are afraid to criticize him. Poor Jedidah is living in fear that her husband will sacrifice Josiah to Molech."

Huldah gave a deep groan. "How *is* the little boy?"

Miriama shook her head. "He's terrified of his father. Whenever Amon comes, Josiah runs to hide."

* * *

As the months passed, Huldah's father and mother came daily to visit her. "I wish you were home with us," complained Abital, "instead of here in this big house."

"This is my home," Huldah answered. "I'll wait here for Shallum to return."

"Who knows when that will happen?" grumbled Barak. "Trade has fallen off again. With no building going on, workmen are idle. More and more of the poor are homeless and hungry. Thieves enter houses or rob people in the streets—I knew this would happen when Amon became king."

After they returned to their house, Huldah settled in front of her hearth. She picked up her embroidery, a large woolen wall hanging she was fashioning for her husband's room. It covered her knees and spread onto the carpeted floor. The wool's warmth felt good on this late autumn day. *Two years already*, she mused. *Two years since Shallum left our home to choose a robe for King Manasseh's burial.*

A gust of wind blew against the wall and whined through a crack. Soon rain spattered against the house.

Early the next morning shouts in the street awakened her. Leaving her room she encountered her servants clustered in the damp courtyard, and she instructed the doorkeeper to find out the reason for the noise. He soon returned, trembling with excitement. "King Amon is dead.

Last night some of his courtiers attacked him with daggers."

"Oh," screamed a maidservant, "no one is safe, not even a king."

"You're right," agreed the doorkeeper. "A mob of citizens is marching right now toward the palace. Rumor is that they want to make sure those men of the court don't kill the entire royal family and other nobles and then seize the power to rule with a new royal line."

"Don't anyone leave this house," advised Huldah. "Here you are safer than in the streets." She returned to her room so they wouldn't see the tears that were seeping into her eyes. Prince Josiah and his little brother. . . Queen Jedidah . . . Miriama . . . Shallum. Danger threatened all of them.

The tears overflowed. "Lord, if only I could talk to Shallum . . ." In sudden illogical determination she reached for her woolen cloak. "I'll go. Yes, I'll go to the palace, and I'll search until I find my husband."

Chapter 9

Ignoring her own better judgment and oblivious to the disapproval of her doorkeeper and warnings from the guards outside the gate, Huldah left the courtyard and headed toward the palace. As she wound through the deserted streets, she became aware of the strange quiet. Only the sound of her sandals on the stones broke the stillness. No shouts filled the marketplace. Merchants had barred the doors of their shops and retreated behind the walls. Her mind raced ahead. *First I'll look for Miriama, and she'll tell me how to find Shallum.*

At the approach to the palace, Huldah paused in shock when she spotted only a few soldiers looking down from the walls. Entering the courtyard, she hurried to the women's garden and found the two Nubians still guarding the entry to the women's quarters. Surprise showed on their faces. "We thought you might never return to the palace," one of them said.

After they allowed her into the building, she ran through the hallway and up the staircase to Jedidah's door.

Without waiting for an invitation, she burst into the reception room.

The queen stood by the window with her hands to the sides of her face. "Huldah! They killed Amon. His courtiers, the ones he trusted. They've seized power and I'm afraid they'll come for my sons."

Huldah drew her to a couch and sat with her arm around the terrified woman. "Where are the boys?"

"I've hidden them in my bedchamber." Jedidah pressed her fists against her eyes. "Amon was only 24 years old. I hoped the Lord would speak to him and change him like He changed his father. Two years was not enough time. Now my hope is gone." She bowed her head and strands of dark hair fell across her face.

Tears came to Huldah's eyes, not for Amon but for her friend.

From somewhere outside the palace, angry shouting rose and fell. Jedidah raised her head. "You must leave immediately. It's not safe for you here. Now that the courtiers have seized power, they'll break into the women's quarters to rid themselves of all the royal family and our servants. There's no need for you to lose your life just because you're my friend. They'll search the women's quarters until they find us."

"What about the secret room beneath the floor? Can't we all hide there?"

"The courtiers know about the room. It's the first place they'd look," Jedidah wailed. "I can't bear to think of what they'll do to my sons."

Huldah walked to the window and peered down into a courtyard but saw no one there. As she searched past the wall to a hillside, the sounds began to recede. Returning to Jedidah, she sat in silence next to the queen. *If only I could find Shallum. He would know what to do.*

Without warning Miriama dashed into the room. "Do you hear all the noise? A mob of citizens overcame the guards at the royal court. They broke down the gates and entered the building. Now they've captured some of the courtiers and are taking them to the Hinnom Valley for execution."

The queen let out a deep breath and lay down on the couch. "All this killing," she moaned. "Now that the citizens have seized power, what will happen next?"

Huldah turned to Miriama and asked anxiously, "Do you have any news of Shallum? I came to find him, but I don't know how."

"I haven't been able to learn anything about him." Miriama replied nervously. "No one responds to my call at the doors to the men's quarters. I don't know what's happened to either my brother or my husband, but I'll keep on trying to find them." After a troubled glance at the prostrate queen, she hurried out.

The door to Jedidah's inner chambers banged open, and Josiah ran into the room. "What's going on? The servants won't tell me anything."

He had grown taller during the two years Huldah had remained in her home. Black hair curled around his ears. His dark brown eyes showed the same apprehension that sounded in his voice.

"You tell him," whispered Jedidah.

"Your father . . . " Huldah began but stopped, not knowing how to relate the news that the boy's father was dead.

Josiah came across the room to stand close to her. "Huldah, I haven't seen you for a long, long time." He looked directly into her eyes. "Did something happen to my father?"

There was no way she could keep the frightening news

from him. "Yes. Some of the courtiers have taken his life."

A frown creased his forehead. "Mother told me that some day he might become a good king, but I guess it's too late for that." He paused before whispering, "I was afraid of him, but I didn't want him to die."

"None of us expected him to die."

Josiah's face took on a look of concentration. "Since my father is no longer king, does that mean that I have to become king right away?"

Wanting to hold him in her arms as she had when he was younger, Huldah restrained herself. She took his hand in hers. "That's the way it usually happens."

Jedidah sat up. "But it might not happen that way this time. We don't know what that mob of citizens will do. Huldah, you must disguise my sons and take them away. Anywhere. Away."

Before Huldah could answer, the door opened and Miriama entered again. "Some of the citizens have returned from the valley, and they're asking to see Josiah."

His mother stood up. "Hide him somewhere. I don't want to lose my son."

"No, they won't harm Josiah. The people are ready to proclaim him the new king."

At that moment noise erupted in the passageway, and someone flung open the door. A large man in a blood-stained robe stepped into the room. "Josiah is king! We've come to take him to the royal court and declare that he is king." A group of men shoved in behind him, and others in the hallway crowded toward them.

Wide-eyed, the boy looked toward his mother. She left her place by the couch and, taking a deep breath, stood composed and regal to face the men. "You will crown my son Josiah in the proper and traditional manner with a priest of the Lord to anoint him."

Astonished, the citizens stared at the slender young queen confronting them. One man found enough courage to speak. "Of course our intentions were honorable, but we transgressed when we invaded your quarters. We will go to the high priest and arrange the proper coronation ceremony for our next king." The men backed out of the room and shouted to the waiting crowd, "To the Temple mount. We must talk to the high priest."

Having spent her energy, Jedidah drooped again onto the couch. From the inner chambers another dark-haired boy, younger than his brother Josiah, raced into the room and scrambled onto the couch next to his mother. He hid his face against her arm.

Josiah stood in front of Jedidah. "As soon as I am king, I'm going to order happy times for everyone."

Running footsteps again sounded in the hallway, and Miriama burst into the room. "I found Enosh, and he told me the guards had released all prisoners. Shallum might be on his way home."

Huldah turned to face the queen. "Then may I leave to go to my husband?"

With her younger son on the couch and Josiah standing by her side, Jedidah spoke softly, "You are dismissed. I still have my two sons to give me comfort."

An uneasy quiet hovered over the streets of Jerusalem. Still wary of mob violence, only a few men and women ventured out of their homes.

As Huldah walked briskly along the nearly deserted streets, her heart beat more rapidly when she thought that Shallum might have arrived home and was waiting for her. Or after two years in the dungeon was he too sick to walk? Could he make it safely through the streets?

Watching for any glimpse of her husband crumpled in a doorway or against a wall, she finally reached their own gate. A manservant opened it for her, and she rushed into the courtyard. "Has the master of the house arrived?"

Smiling, the servant pointed to Shallum's room, "He's there."

As Huldah hurried across the courtyard, a pale man with an unkempt gray beard stepped out of the room. When he limped forward, she realized it was Shallum. Abruptly she stopped to stare at him. He reached out to her with thin hands, and she stepped toward him until his arms encircled her. "Shallum, Shallum," she whispered.

His voice was low and husky. "The servants said you went to look for me."

"And I've found you in our own home." Huldah placed her arm around his waist and steered him into the warmth of his room. "I was afraid that if either the courtiers or the people of the city took you, I'd never see you again." She pressed her head against his shoulder, and her tears spilled onto his musty, ragged robe. "What did they do to you in that prison? You're so thin and you're limping."

He held her close. "Two years in a dungeon takes away strength, but now that I'm home with you, I'll recover."

"Yes, you're home," she whispered, thinking that after two years of days and nights without him, now she was home again in his arms. She lifted her head from his shoulder and waited for his kiss. It came soft and gentle on her waiting lips. Then he smiled down at her and kissed her again, more eagerly this time.

When knocking sounded at the gate and a servant crossed the courtyard to open it, Shallum's body tensed and he stared suspiciously into the courtyard. Seeing only their doorkeeper enter, he left the room to talk to the man. "What's the latest news?"

The doorkeeper's face brightened into a broad smile. "Welcome home, Master Shallum. I learned in the streets that the citizens released you from prison."

"Tell me the news," demanded Shallum. "What about these citizens? Have they returned to their homes?"

The doorkeeper shook his head. "Not yet. They're up on the Temple mount conferring with the high priest Hilkiah."

"What business have they with Hilkiah?"

"They're asking him to proclaim Josiah as king."

Turning to Huldah who was standing behind him, Shallum asked, "Soldiers would tell me nothing, but people in the streets said that Amon is dead. Is this true?"

"It's true," she replied and then watched her husband silently ponder the news.

At last he spoke. "Josiah is only eight years old. There are always groups of citizens or nobles or priests who would like to seize power for themselves. Can we trust anyone? Outside enemies will hear about Judah's boy king and consider this a good time to invade. Who will come first? Assyrians, Babylonians, Chaldeans, or Egyptians?" He limped to the door of his room. "As soon as I'm able, I'll go to the royal court and offer my services to Josiah."

The doorkeeper entered the menservants' quarters, and Huldah stood alone in the courtyard.

"Can we trust anyone?" she repeated. Remembering the young queen facing the mob of citizens, Huldah felt confident that from his mother's side of the family, strong blood flowed in Josiah's veins. She would trust the righteousness that Jedidah had already imparted and would continue to inspire in the boy king.

But he was still only a little boy with designing men—some unscrupulous and crafty—surrounding him. Huldah looked up at the gloomy winter sky. "Lord God, she prayed, "guard this child and the great task that lies ahead of him."

Two days later dressed in a clean robe and with his gray beard neatly trimmed, Shallum announced, "Today I will go to the royal court."

Eager to see Josiah, Huldah asked, "May I go with you?"

As they strolled through the streets, Shallum reached for his wife's hand. "This is like the old times when I escorted you to the palace."

She smiled in remembrance, and yet a feeling of uneasiness crept over her. The city remained too quiet, and she noticed that only a few shoppers headed toward the marketplace. She looked up at the sky. A westerly wind blowing somber clouds suggested the return of rain.

They entered through one of the southern gates and made their way up to the royal court. Miriama's husband, Enosh, stood guard outside the king's reception room. "Many officials are waiting to speak to Josiah, but I'll let you in next. He's been asking for you."

He rapped with the hilt of his sword on the door. When a soldier cautiously opened it, Huldah's gaze was drawn immediately to the boy seated on the high ivory throne. A wave of concern washed over her. Josiah leaned against silken cushions and appeared tired. How small he looked on that big throne with his feet dangling above the floor.

Scribes sat at tables, and courtiers clustered on both sides of the throne. Hilkiah, the high priest, stood near the king. Some of the courtiers whispered among themselves and glanced distrustfully at Shallum.

Chapter 10

When he saw his visitors, Josiah's eyes brightened and he sat up straighter.

Shallum was the first to speak. "I have come to offer my services to our new king."

A smile livened the boy's face. "That's good." He leaned toward the high priest, and they conferred for a few moments. "Hilkiah is my advisor," Josiah explained. "We think you should be the keeper of my wardrobe just like you were for my grandfather."

Shallum bowed to the young king. "The honor is mine."

Josiah's gaze rested on Huldah. "I want you to come to the palace too."

She bowed her head and offered, "I could open my school for the ladies again."

Hilkiah spoke with Josiah. The boy turned to Huldah. "My advisor thinks you should teach in the palace and also sit at the city center to interpret messages from the Lord. That's what I want you to do." He slipped off the throne and stood looking up at the priest. "And right now I want to go to the garden and play with my dog."

The courtier Zophar stepped forward. "But, my lord, many officials are waiting to see you."

Hilkiah faced him. "I have anointed Josiah as king. If he wishes to go to the garden to play with his dog, he may go."

Josiah marched to the door and ordered the doorkeepers to open it. Before leaving he turned around. "Shallum and Huldah, come with me."

The king's garden lay close to the palace. Twenty-five stone steps led up to the wall that separated this garden from the Temple mount. Huldah and Shallum sat together on a bench. Clouds unraveled to let in the winter sunshine, and blue of the heavens reflected in the garden's pool.

Enosh opened a door, and the pharaoh hound darted into the garden. With Josiah running after him, they raced around the paths until the dog panted to a stop in front of Huldah.

Josiah wrinkled his nose. "It's no fun just to sit on a throne all day. I like to play once in awhile." He raised his head. "I hear something." Dashing away, he climbed the steps to the gate in the Temple mount's wall.

Alarmed, Shallum hurried after him. Together they descended, and Josiah called to Enosh, "I heard a boy's voice in the Temple courtyard. Go find out who he is and bring him to me." When he spoke to Huldah, his eyes danced in happy anticipation. "I have only my little brother to play with, but maybe I can have a friend too." He squatted on the path with his arm around the dog.

Enosh entered the garden, pushing a squirming child in front of him. "Here's the boy. His father's a priest, a Benjaminite from Anathoth. He comes once a year to take his turn offering sacrifices in the Temple. This year he brought his son along."

"My name is Jeremiah," shouted the boy.

A Benjaminite from Anathoth. Remembering the night that Shallum tried to kidnap Josiah and take him away, Huldah glanced at her husband.

"I know his father, this priest from Anathoth," he said. "He's a good man."

Jeremiah stopped squirming and glared at the hound. "I've never seen a dog like that before. He doesn't look like one of those mean, wild dogs that run around in packs."

"He's not mean. He's a pharaoh hound," Josiah explained. "When I became king, my mother gave me her dog."

"What's his name?"

"Nebka."

"Is that an Egyptian dog? Egyptians are bad."

"Their dogs are good. Come on, I'll show you." He darted away with the dog at his heels.

For a moment Jeremiah hesitated. Then he ran after the king and his pet.

Enosh laughed. "I think the court session is finished for today. The officials will have to wait."

Huldah glanced up at one of the windows overlooking the garden. She recognized lean, dark-eyed Zophar and another courtier scowling at the boys as they played with Josiah's dog. Although she couldn't hear what the men were saying, the sound of their voices conveyed annoyance. She touched her husband's arm. "The courtiers are not happy with our new king."

Shallum dragged his attention away from the boys and the dog. "Why can't they give him a chance?" he grumbled. "He'll show he's not like his father."

Huldah shook her head. "I'm afraid they want all the power for themselves."

Enosh surveyed the windows. "I'll assign a strong group of soldiers to guard Josiah." Speaking directly to Shallum, he added, "Since you're keeper of his wardrobe, you will spend time with him each day and can watch over him in his private chambers."

And who'll watch over my husband? Huldah wondered.

* * *

Now when Huldah accompanied Shallum outside the city walls to carry water to travelers, she noticed that he proceeded cautiously at the gate and wherever one of Zophar's followers might lurk. Walking to the palace, he slowed his pace at each turn in the streets. One day a large stone fell from the top of a wall, barely missing Shallum's head. When Enosh found out, he ordered extra soldiers to patrol the streets through which Shallum and Huldah passed. And so the months went by and then the years without further mishaps.

As for Josiah, with soldiers to protect him even as he walked through the palace halls, the boy king avoided calamity and retained the throne.

Each spring the almond trees in the king's garden unfolded their scented blossoms. One spring day Josiah sat alone in the garden except for his dog and two guards who stood by the door to a passageway, but he didn't notice the almonds' fragrance. The pharaoh hound sprawled on the bench beside him while Josiah held its slender head in his lap. The dog breathed heavily and with difficulty.

One of the guards opened the door to allow Enosh to enter. Josiah looked up. "I told the guards to let no one near me until after my dog dies."

"Please forgive me," replied Enosh. "Your friend Jeremiah has just arrived from the north. He was so eager to see you, he came in his traveling clothes and has managed to talk his way past all the guards. Right now he's standing at the door to this garden."

"If Jeremiah can do that, let him in."

When his friend strode toward him, Josiah managed to give him a faint smile. "I'm glad you came."

Jeremiah knelt by the dog and stroked its back. "What's wrong with Nebka?"

"My doctors say he's old and tired . . . and ready to die."

"I'll wait with you." He situated himself at the other end of the bench. They sat quietly, saying little. In the distance, migrating turtledoves crooned their wistful calls. Nearer, in the stables, horses stomped. The pharaoh hound breathed softly one last time. Josiah smoothed the fur on its head.

Jeremiah placed his hand on the dog's back. "We'll miss him. My father says that when death strikes, we must turn to the Lord for comfort."

"That's what Huldah says too."

After the servants wrapped the hound's body in linen strips and buried it under one of the garden's almond trees, Jeremiah again sat with his friend. Josiah was the first to speak. "The high priest Hilkiah has been advising me to take a wife."

"A wife! Do you want to?"

Josiah shrugged his shoulders. "I don't know, but now that I'm almost 16, I guess it's time. Hilkiah says it's good to strengthen our ties with the outlying districts. He suggested a girl named Hamutal of Libnah."

"Have you ever seen her? Is she pretty?"

"I haven't seen her. Hilkiah says that's not important. What we need, besides gaining support from all of Judah, is to continue following the wishes of the courtiers and the citizens of Jerusalem." Josiah paused to think deeply before he added, "I need to ask Huldah's advice."

"Huh!" Jeremiah snorted. "How come you're always asking Huldah's advice?"

Josiah stood up. "I ask her advice because I trust her. Don't listen to what the courtiers and some of the priests say. They don't like Huldah because she's been telling me to get rid of the altars to Baal and other foreign idols." His voice grew calmer. "As soon as I can, I'm going to start reforms in this kingdom."

Jeremiah's voice revealed his excitement. "My father says you should get rid of all the altars and also the high places, where priests sacrifice to foreign idols. When are you going to start doing it?"

Josiah frowned in deep concentration. "The Assyrians aren't as strong as they were when they took my grandfather away, but we still have to watch out for the Babylonians and the Egyptians."

Jeremiah jumped to his feet. "Fight them. Fight them."

"First, I guess I'd better marry that girl from Libnah."

* * *

A few days later Huldah came home early from teaching the ladies in the palace. Although the afternoon was warm and sunshine still touched the courtyard wall, she hugged her cloak more tightly to her body. Preoccupied with the news she had heard, she was only dimly aware of the aroma of bread baking and the rattling of pots and dishes as the cooks prepared the evening meal.

At last the welcome sound of Shallum's footsteps echoed in the street. When he entered the courtyard, she ran to him. "I must talk to you."

He put his arm around her shoulders. "Is what you have to talk about so important that it can't wait until after the evening meal?"

Chapter 11

Miriama told me that Josiah is going to be married,"
Huldah blurted, "and Hilkiah has advised him
to take not only one wife but two."

"Come and sit down." Shallum led her to a couch in his
room. "That's not unusual. Most kings marry more than one
woman."

She leaned against him. "Yes, I know that's true, but
Josiah is so young. It's hard enough to lose him to this girl
Hamutal but the other one is Zebidah. She's two years
older than Josiah."

"He's no longer a little boy," her husband gently
reminded her, "and we have to remember that he's not
our son. These brides come from outer territories, and
Hilkiah realizes we must strengthen Jerusalem's ties with
these districts. We need them to help resist attack from
Babylon or Egypt." He tightened his embrace. "But foreign
powers are not the only threats to Josiah."

Huldah stiffened and raised her head from his shoulder. "What do you mean?"

"Josiah talks of making reforms, of destroying all the foreign idols and their altars." Shallum stood up and faced his wife. "But Zophar and his followers are stirring up opposition. He's telling the citizens this could bring on an invasion."

Huldah held her hands over her eyes. "Since Josiah was a little boy, I've told him that the Temple needs repair and that the people of Judah should stop worshiping idols. I didn't think his own courtiers would turn against him. What can such a young king do?"

"He can at least marry those girls from the territories of Libnah and Rumah."

She took a deep breath and sighed, "If this is the only way to strengthen the kingdom, I suppose I must accept it."

* * *

During the following month, the people of Jerusalem prepared for the marriage of King Josiah to Hamutal. The rhythmic notes of flutes and the percussion of cymbals filled the air while musicians practiced their songs. Women and girls went out to the hills and gathered palm branches, yellow daisies, and a variety of lilies to decorate the city. The morning of the wedding, wealthy citizens donned their finest robes and draped golden chains around their necks. Even beggars washed their faces and hands for the festive occasion.

In the women's quarters of the palace, Hamutal's mother and the court ladies adorned the bride in a silk gown, golden in color and festooned with rows of emeralds and pearls.

Huldah sat in the queen's reception room with Jedidah and Miriama.

"Soon everyone will know me as queen *mother*," Jedidah said softly.

Miriama shook her head. "You will always remain our queen." Huldah nodded in agreement.

The piping of flutes and beat of cymbals indicated that Josiah was coming for his bride. Jedidah, Huldah, and Miriama followed Hamutal and her attendants into the women's garden, where the groom waited. A lump caught in Huldah's throat as she watched the bride's father remove the veil that covered Hamutal's face and place it on Josiah's shoulder.

Flanked by a strong guard of armed soldiers and attended by men and women of the court, the king and his bride went out to parade through Jerusalem's streets. Then they returned to the palace, where music and feasting continued far into the night.

A month later Josiah ordered all these festivities repeated for his marriage to Zebidah. Along with Jedidah and Miriama, Huldah again listened to the flutes and cymbals. She watched the bride, who was dressed in a blue silk gown decorated with discs of gold, step regally forward to her groom.

Josiah's mother wiped tears from her eyes. Huldah and Miriama put their arms around her and led her back to her chambers.

* * *

Nearly a year passed before Jeremiah returned to Jerusalem. Immediately he sought out the young king. Guards allowed him to enter the royal court and wait in the smallest reception room.

As soon as Josiah came in, Jeremiah confronted him. "I thought you said you were going to make some reforms.

When are you going to begin?"

Josiah closed the door to the passageway, shutting out the guards who waited there. "I want to be a good king like my ancestor David, but I have to proceed slowly. Some of the courtiers are against any reforms, and if I act too quickly, they might try to seize control."

"Looks to me like all you've done so far is provide a couple of heirs to the throne."

"Now that I have a son with each of my wives, my enemies are more eager than ever to rid themselves of the royal family."

"Enosh and his guards are loyal to you, and the high priest wants to throw out the idols," Jeremiah snorted. "What are you waiting for?"

Josiah raised his voice. "For the right time."

"When?" shouted Jeremiah.

Josiah tapped his friend on the shoulder. "You're beginning to shout like a prophet."

"Not me. Just because I'm loud doesn't mean I'm going to become a prophet. I wouldn't want to be one."

"You sure sound like one."

Jeremiah walked to a window and gazed out to the southern hills. "Huldah's a prophet, but she doesn't shout."

Josiah joined him at the window. "God uses people in different ways. Huldah works in her own quiet way. Right now she's helping me study the scrolls we have so I can find out what the Lord wants me to do. You could go out in the streets and shout. What are you waiting for?"

"Like you, for the right time." Jeremiah pressed his lips together.

* * *

Up in the palace Huldah finished the reading lesson for

the day. As the ladies filed out the doorway, she placed the library scrolls on a shelf in her schoolroom. A few minutes later she joined Jedidah in the queen mother's chambers. A maidservant brought dates and almonds and offered them to Huldah. While she munched the fruit and nuts, her attention focused on Jedidah.

The queen mother twisted her hands together and stared at the floor. Finally she looked up. "I'm concerned about Josiah."

Huldah made an effort to keep her reply calm. "In what way?"

"I'm proud of my son. Even though he's young, he makes wise decisions, but now he's determined to begin those reforms, to cleanse the Temple of foreign idols and their altars." Jedidah shook her head. "Isn't that what I've wanted? Isn't that what you and I have hoped he would do? Now that he says he will, why am I terrified?"

Before Huldah could answer, a maidservant announced that the king had arrived to visit his mother. The women stood up to greet the young man. *How handsome he is!* Huldah mused. *Tall and slender like his father, but he has the thick dark hair and slightly darker skin from his mother's clan.* The start of a beard showed on his face.

He strode in and kissed Jedidah on both cheeks and then kissed Huldah. Seating himself on a couch, he announced, "I've come to inform you of my plans." At his words, sudden fear stabbed Huldah. She looked toward the door, wishing to escape even the knowledge of what he proposed to undertake.

On the opposite couch, Jedidah drew in a shaky breath. "We're listening. Please tell us."

"We can't go on forever allowing some priests to offer sacrifices to foreign idols. And the Temple itself is in terrible condition. Gold falls from the ceiling and disappears. For years cracks have appeared in the walls and the floor. New materials are needed." Josiah stood up and pounded his right fist into his other hand. "I'm going to order repairs."

"How will you pay for these repairs?" his mother asked.

"Taxes. I'll have to tax the people of Judah."

"They won't like more taxes."

"I know," replied her son thoughtfully. "That's why I must proceed slowly—just a little increase at a time. We'll save the silver and gold that's collected until we have enough to start repairing the Temple and removing the idols."

Huldah swallowed hard. "You must take great care. Zophar and his followers will never agree to these reforms."

Josiah sighed. "You're right. But I would rather follow what God wants me to do than what some men want." He smiled at Jedidah and Huldah. "Isn't that what you have taught me for as long as I can remember?"

The women looked at each other but said nothing.

"When we have collected enough silver to pay their wages," Josiah continued, "we can hire carpenters, builders, and masons. We'll need to buy timber and quarry stone. Gold we'll use to beautify the Temple. All this may take a few years, but I assure you we shall have reform in Judah while I am king. I will no longer serve the interests of foreign powers nor my own subjects who wish to serve them."

He rose from the couch and stepped close to his mother. Taking her hands in his, he spoke softly, "Don't worry. God is with us." He smiled reassuringly at Huldah and left the room.

The women sat in stunned silence until Huldah said, "Josiah's plans are right and good."

"Yes, but at what price?" Jedidah sobbed. "With what danger to Josiah?"

* * *

During the summer the young king sent town criers into the streets of Jerusalem to announce that he was increasing taxes. Messengers rode out to all parts of Judah to inform the people that Josiah needed money to repair the Temple.

"Why should we send our silver and gold to Jerusalem?" some grumbled. "We can worship at the high places in our own territory."

Others disagreed. "Finally we have a good king who is ruling like his ancestor David. We will do as he asks."

* * *

At her booth in the marketplace one afternoon, Huldah prepared to return home. Many citizens had sought her counsel that day, asking that she inquire of the Lord about paying extra taxes to repair the Temple. As she stepped out of the booth, a familiar figure walked toward her. Even after all these years of marriage, her heart still gave a leap of excitement when she saw Shallum in the marketplace.

"Will you walk with me to the Mount of Olives on this lovely summer afternoon?"

She touched his hand. "I will."

Outside the walls, they strolled into the Kidron Valley and wandered part way up the mount. An old shepherd woman sat quietly watching a few sheep. Near her, two small boys played with stones and sticks.

Farther along the hillside Huldah and Shallum found a

comfortable resting place under the gray-green leaves of a young olive tree.

Sitting close together in comfortable silence, they gazed across the valley. A soft breeze brought the pungent scent of thyme blossoms. As she admired Solomon's Temple and the beloved city of Jerusalem, words from one of her scrolls came to mind. "How lovely is thy dwelling place, O Lord of hosts."

Becoming aware of the little boys calling to each other, Huldah said, "I'm sorry."

Puzzled, Shallum looked at her. "Why are you sorry on a beautiful day like this?"

"Because I've given you no sons, not even a daughter. You'll never have grandsons."

He laid his hand against her cheek to turn her face toward his. "We have Josiah—at least in our hearts we have him."

"Josiah," she echoed but could say no more. And then she heard a whimper, a faint sound from somewhere on the hill behind them. Something was crying. She twisted around to find the source of the noise. From a bush a small brown puppy tumbled down the hillside and landed in Huldah's lap. It looked up at her with big brown eyes. Wiggling to its feet it jumped up to lick her face.

Shallum chuckled. "This little animal likes you."

Trying to calm the excited puppy, Huldah held it in her arms and stroked its back. "It probably belongs to those boys. I'll take it to them."

When the shepherd woman saw Huldah with the dog, she looked the other way.

"Is this your puppy?" Huldah asked.

"No, it's a stray. I don't want it. I have enough to care for with my sheep and my grandsons."

The little dog's eyes pleaded with Huldah. "You're so thin," she said.

Shallum patted its head. "Shall we take him home with us?"

She wrapped the end of her shawl around the puppy and hugged it to her. "Since keeping dogs is an Egyptian custom, they're not welcome in the city." She shook her head. "But if we leave this one here, he'll starve."

"I know a couple of city officials who have dogs."

The puppy squirmed and Huldah tightened her hold. "Let's keep him."

All the way to the city and through the streets, she cuddled the warm puppy under her shawl and planned where she might make a bed for it in her room.

But when they stopped at their courtyard gate, her attention shifted from the little dog to the anxious face of the doorkeeper. Before they could enter the courtyard, he informed Shallum, "A messenger arrived to say that you are wanted in the king's royal court immediately."

Chapter 12

At this time of day!" exclaimed Huldah.

"If Josiah needs me, I must go," her husband replied.

"Yes of course," she agreed, but as soon as he went out the gate, she wanted to call him back. Perhaps Josiah had not sent the message.

At the royal court Shallum followed the sounds of angry voices to the large reception room, where Josiah sat rigidly on the ivory throne.

Zophar's loud words carried above the noisy gathering. "If we remove idols and their altars from the Temple, we can expect to receive the wrath of foreign powers."

"If we do not remove them," replied Josiah, "we can expect to receive the wrath of God."

The authoritative voice of the high priest Hilkiah quieted the assembly. "The time has come to cleanse the Temple."

In support of the king and the priest, Shallum spoke. "When enough money has come in for needed repairs to the Temple, many men will have work. With wages to stonemasons, carpenters, and other artisans, we can expect a time of prosperity."

Zophar's fierce eyes glared at Shallum. "What about the royal court? If the Temple can have gold on the ceiling, why can't the court have it too?" He turned to Josiah. "Prosperity will come just as easily if you divert tax money for courtiers to use."

Josiah stood up and pulled himself as tall as possible. "I will follow the counsel of my advisor Hilkiah. The time has come to remove the idols and repair the Temple. I, your king, have spoken." He raised his hand. "All of you except Hilkiah have my permission to leave. The high priest and I will formulate plans."

Zophar shot a glance, angry and threatening, at Shallum. Deliberately ignoring Zophar's hostility, Shallum turned away. Then with all the courtiers and priests except Hilkiah, he backed out of the room.

The king sat down on the throne with the high priest standing next to him.

Seven days later riders left Jerusalem for all parts of Judah, advising the people about an additional increase in taxes to repair the Temple. Over the next months silver and gold accumulated slowly. Temple doorkeepers collected the tax money, and Hilkiah placed it in a large storage chest. He ordered his most trusted guards to watch over it in an underground chamber.

As spring changed to summer and then to autumn, citizens came to Huldah and demanded, "When will Josiah start hiring workers for repair of the Temple?"

"I only interpret messages from the Lord," she told each one. "I don't know when our king will begin his reforms."

While the people grumbled, other springs passed.

Returning home one afternoon, Huldah watched the dog bound across the stones to welcome her. She and Shallum had named him Yaphe and with infinite patience had trained him to obey. Now the large, brown mongrel sat down and waited for her to rub behind his long ears and over his backbone.

Huldah knelt to pat him. When she walked to her room, he followed her and lay down near her hearth. She removed her cloak and put away the papyrus that she had carried with her. Hearing her husband at the gate, she instructed Yaphe, "Go to Shallum."

He raced out of the room and across the courtyard. Smiling, Huldah stood in the doorway to observe the dog's exuberant greeting of his master.

After giving Yaphe a pat, Shallum hurried across the courtyard to his wife.

Observing his quick stride, her smile faded and misgiving seized her. "Has something happened to Josiah?"

"Just the opposite. Today he ordered the priests to remove one of Baal's altars from the Temple. Nubian slaves have hammered it into pieces so they can carry the heavy stone." He started toward the gate. "Come with me and we'll go out to watch them dump the pieces."

Huldah followed him to the gate. "At last! At last the time is here."

In the street other citizens were headed toward the northern gate. "The word has spread," said Shallum.

"Wait!" Huldah stopped walking. "Why is everyone going this way? Shouldn't we be going to the Hinnom? That's where King Manasseh threw the altars and idols when he cleansed the Temple."

"No. Josiah ordered his slaves to carry the altar to the northern part of the Kidron where the valley is wider and not as steep."

"I've always considered the Hinnom the valley of evil and the Kidron the valley of good."

"Don't worry," advised her husband. "After the slaves have hammered this altar to dust, the Kidron will remain as good as ever."

"Perhaps some day," mused Huldah, "it will even have a brook running through it."

Outside the wall and following a wide path, they arrived at a place where it sloped downward. "There they are," exclaimed Shallum, "and they've already started to beat the pieces into dust." Slaves and soldiers worked side by side, pounding at the stones.

Huldah grabbed her husband's arm. "There's Josiah!"

"He's watching to make sure that nothing but dust will remain of that altar."

She sighed contentedly. "A good king, always doing what is right in the eyes of the Lord."

A woman standing near her spoke up. "But not in the sight of the enemies of Judah."

Shallum placed his hand on top of Huldah's, giving warmth and reassurance.

The sound of pounding continued. Dust drifted, bringing with it the smell of ashes from the many sacrifices the priests of Baal had burned on the stone. The sun set and the blue of the western sky turned soft orange. Torches appeared in the Kidron and work continued. "They will stay until nothing remains," said Shallum. "We can go home, knowing that Josiah will make sure it happens."

From that day, workmen, soldiers, and priests continued to remove the altars of the Baals, their incense stands, and the poles and images of Asherah.

"Beat them into dust," the king ordered, "and strew that dust over the tombs of those who have sacrificed to these idols."

That spring and summer, Josiah, along with Enosh and a contingent of soldiers, rode to the outer territories of Judah. They directed their horses from one high place to another to oversee the destruction of pagan worship.

In Jerusalem's marketplace, Huldah looked up from the scroll she was reading to see Jeremiah standing at the door to her booth. Although three years younger than Josiah and not as tall, he had grown into a sturdy young man.

"I've left Anathoth, and now I live at Solomon's Temple, " he announced.

"Will you come in and tell me more?"

He sat on a bench across the table from her and frowned at the wall. "The Lord is calling me to become a prophet, but how can I? I'm too young, and I'd rather be a priest like my father. I didn't mind shouting at Josiah about how slow he was to start cleansing the country of idols. He's my friend. But where can I find words to shout at other people?"

Remembering Shallum's advice to her many years before, Huldah repeated it for this troubled young man. "If the Lord has chosen you to prophesy, you must accept."

"Why does He need me? I can't speak well enough. He already has the prophets Zephaniah and Nahum in Judah, and they both speak better than I can."

"He will put words into your mouth."

Jeremiah sat silently looking at the floor before he spoke doubtfully. "If I did prophesy, where would He want me to begin?"

Huldah glanced at the steady stream of shoppers passing in the street. "Right here in the marketplace. Even when all the images and altars are gone, in their hearts some Judeans will still worship false gods." She reached across the table and touched his arm. "The Lord has called you to admonish the people and warn them of destruction if they continue in their evil ways."

After hesitating for a moment Jeremiah determined, "I'll do it." He pushed into the crowd of shoppers, and his voice rang out. "Thus says the Lord. 'My people have changed their glory for useless things. My people have done two evils. They have forsaken Me, the source of living waters, and they have dug cisterns for themselves—broken cisterns that hold no water.' "

Huldah saw people staring at Jeremiah, and some backed away from him. She closed her eyes and raised her head. "Thank You, Lord, for this young prophet." Opening her eyes she saw a man standing at her door.

"Who's that out here shouting at us?" he demanded to know.

Huldah stood up to face him. "He is Judah's newest prophet."

The man shook his head and walked away.

* * *

During the next six years, King Josiah continued his search throughout the land for evidences of pagan worship. At the same time, he directed workmen to proceed with repairs in the Temple. Yet in the outlying districts, the people still burned incense to foreign gods, and secretly some of Jerusalem's citizens worshiped idols.

One summer morning Huldah relaxed in her courtyard before walking to the marketplace. Embroidering on a new woolen shawl, she thrust a bone needle through the white woven fabric, stitching a floral design with red, yellow, and green yarn.

Near her feet Yaphe lolled comfortably on the warm courtyard stones. At the sound of hurrying footsteps in the street, he raised his head and growled. A voice at the gate rang out, "Open for the high priest Hilkiah."

The dog barked. Huldah leaned toward him. "Quiet," she said while motioning for a maid to take the dog into the servants' quarters. She laid her embroidery on the bench and stood up to welcome this distinguished visitor to her home. But why hadn't he talked to Shallum at the palace? Her heart pounded in fear. Had something so drastic happened that even the high priest would come to inform her? She adjusted her lightweight yellow robe and smoothed her hair with both hands.

The doorkeeper swung open the heavy gate. "Welcome to the house of Shallum, keeper of the king's wardrobe, and Huldah, the prophetess."

Hilkiah marched in, and four men followed him. Huldah recognized the scribe Shaphan and his son with two other officials from Josiah's court. The priest greeted her. "Peace."

She bowed to him. "Peace. I'm sorry my husband is not at home to receive your call, but please enter his reception chamber. I'll instruct the cooks to prepare refreshments for you to partake while a servant runs to the palace to inform my husband that you are waiting for him." She motioned for a manservant to show the guests into the receiving room.

"Wait! Don't waste our time with refreshments." Hilkiah's demand checked her from entering the kitchen. "We will sit in Shallum's reception chamber, but we have not come here to speak with him. We are here to talk to you." The men strode across the courtyard and into the room that the servant indicated.

To me? Huldah wondered. *These important men have come all the way to my home to talk to me?* She followed them into the room.

Hilkiah sat formally on a carved oak chair. His elaborate robe, woven with golden threads through it, draped over his ample frame. In his hands he held a scroll yellowed with age. The four officials stood behind him.

He cleared his throat. "As you know, those of us who are Levites have been collecting and guarding silver and gold for restoring the Temple. Yesterday after we paid wages to carpenters and builders and masons, I found a large scroll in the bottom of the storage chest." He shifted uneasily on his chair. "I don't know who hid it in that place."

Huldah took a step forward, eager to read what the scroll contained, but instead of handing it to her, the high priest continued to explain. "I showed it to the scribe Shaphan, who read it to the king." Hilkiah shook his head and ordered, "Shaphan, tell Josiah's reaction."

The scribe stood up. "When he heard the words, our king tore his clothes and moaned that the wrath of God is kindled against us. Then he appointed the five of us to carry the scroll to you for further interpretation."

Hilkiah held out the large roll of papyrus toward her. "Read it now so that we can return to King Josiah with your prophecy."

With eager hands she reached for the scroll. Brittle with age, it felt light and vulnerable. She placed it on a side table and unrolled the first section. For a moment Huldah was sensitive to the men watching her, but when she began to read, nothing entered her mind except the Lord's words that an ancient scribe had recorded.

His writing warns of consequences whenever people depart from worship of the Lord, Huldah reflected silently. *This law book curses the disobedient with doom. How true it is that our people are as disloyal to God today as at any time in our history!*

After reading the entire scroll, she remained in deep thought with her chin cupped in her hand. The words she had read were not just history. They were holy words. God's true revelation. Her eyes widened in sudden insight. For many years she had read scrolls without realizing that the words were truly sacred. Only today, from this book of law, the Lord revealed to her that she was reading Holy Scripture.

Hilkiah's voice reached into her consciousness. "What do you understand from these writings?"

Slowly she stood up and faced him. "You have brought Holy Scripture for me to interpret. Tell King Josiah that the Lord says, 'Because they have forsaken Me and have burned incense unto others gods, I will bring evil upon this place and upon the inhabitants thereof. My wrath shall be kindled against this place, and shall not be quenched.'"

The priest turned pale. He grabbed the neck of his robe as if to tear it. Instead he lowered his hands to the arm of the chair and heaved himself to his feet.

"Please wait," begged Huldah. "There is more to the message." She bowed her head, unable to continue.

"Hurry and tell me so I can report to the king," insisted Hilkiah.

With great effort she composed herself enough to speak. "It's too late for the people of Judah, yet for our king the Lord says, 'Because you have humbled yourself and torn your clothes and wept before Me, I have heard you. Therefore I will gather you to your grave in peace. Your eyes shall not see all the evil which I will bring upon this place.'"

For a moment Hilkiah stared at Huldah. Then he picked up the scroll. "So be it. I will inform King Josiah." Solemnly he walked out the door and across the courtyard. The other men followed.

Huldah dropped to her knees and bent her head to the floor. "Lord," she groaned, "why have the inhabitants of

Judah brought this disaster upon the land so that Josiah must die while still young?" Finding no answer to her question, she stood up and told herself, "Now I must go to my booth in the marketplace."

When she walked across the courtyard to the gate, the dog ran out of the servants' quarters. Looking up with eager brown eyes, he asked to go with her.

"No," she cautioned, "you can't go with me. Wait here for Shallum. When he comes, he'll take you for a run along the Kidron Valley."

Sadly the dog lay down to wait.

In the city center, the shopkeepers called out their wares. "Pomegranates, pomegranates. Nice and ripe. Ready to eat." "Fresh dates. Just arrived from the south."

The familiar scene and the people in it appeared peaceful, harmless. Yet after reading the scroll from the Temple, Huldah sensed anew the evil in their hearts. Even Jeremiah's loud warnings went unheeded.

She entered her booth in the marketplace, and while waiting for citizens to come for advice, she sat down to read the words of Isaiah from a papyrus she carried with her. "For you have forgotten the God of your salvation, and have not remembered the Rock of your refuge." The prophet Isaiah had given this warning more than 100 years before. Now she and Jeremiah must repeat it. Some time after midday the shouting of town criers echoed throughout the marketplace. "King Josiah has declared that tomorrow before the sun is high, all citizens must assemble on the Temple mount. Each and every one must come."

Men crowded into Huldah's booth. "Why has the king summoned us to the Temple mount?" "What does this mean?"

"King Josiah will inform us tomorrow," was all she would tell them.

The following morning Huldah and Shallum walked together through the city streets. She glanced at him. "How many years have passed since we took Josiah here?"

"Twenty-six years ago we brought him to the priest for redemption. How much our life has revolved around him all this time!"

"And now we're with him again on the Temple mount." Her voice shook. "But this time he's here to tell the people about their unredeemed sin."

Shallum held her hand while they climbed the path to the mount. After passing through the gate, they saw that a crowd had already gathered.

"I'll have to leave you here," explained Shallum. "Josiah plans to stand by a pillar on the Temple porch and has asked me and some of his most trusted officials to stay near him." He threaded his way through the rapidly growing crowd.

Near Huldah the limestone Temple rose high. As she walked slowly forward, the voices of the people around her faded away. She was aware only of this sacred place. Although she had never seen the inside of the building, she knew there was beauty in the Holy of Holies, where two cherubim guarded the precious Ark of the Covenant.

Someone bumped into her, and she felt rough hands on her arm. "Stop," a voice hissed. "Go no farther."

Chapter 13

Zophar! Take your hands off my arm."

"Not until you hear what I have to say." Huldah tried to pull away but his grip proved too strong. He pushed his face close to hers. "The king should have taken that scroll to a prophet, not a woman who claims to be one. Now he plans to honor you by telling your interpretation to all of Jerusalem. I'm warning you. Stop this prophesying, and tell Shallum to give up his position in the court. If you don't do as I say, dire consequences lie ahead for you, your husband, and the king." With a last threatening glance at her, he forced his way through the crowd until she could no longer see him.

Shaken from the encounter, Huldah edged forward until the crowd blocked her way. When she raised herself onto her toes, she could see Josiah dressed in a purple robe richly decorated with golden embroidery. Shallum, wearing a robe of brown and white stripes, stood behind him on the Temple porch. She caught a glimpse of Jeremiah on the other side. Miriama and Queen Mother

Jedidah waited at the front of the crowd with Josiah's wives and children. Searching through the multitude, Huldah finally spotted her father, mother, and Kezia standing together.

How soon could she talk to her husband? Huldah ached to know. How soon could she warn him about Zophar's threat?

The king's voice rang out for the people to hear. "Our high priest, Hilkiah, has found a scroll that someone stored in the Temple many years ago." While Josiah read the scroll to them, the citizens listened with growing agitation. The sun climbed higher into the sky, and still the words of destruction pounded at them. ". . .You shall serve your enemies whom the Lord will send against you. . . . And the Lord will scatter you among all peoples, from one end of the earth to the other. . . . And there shall be no rest for the sole of your foot. . . ."

Handing the scroll to a waiting courtier, the king announced, "Yesterday I ordered Hilkiah to take the book to the prophetess Huldah for interpretation. She has informed me that this writing is Holy Scripture." When he disclosed her prediction that God would bring evil upon them, the people broke into great wailing and lamentation.

Josiah lifted his hand for silence. "Today I am making a covenant before the Lord. I will keep His commandments and His testimonies and His statutes. With all my heart and with all my soul, I will perform the words of the covenant that are written in this book. From this day forward I will remove the abominations out of the land. All the people will serve the Lord their God, and Him only will they serve."

After pausing briefly, Josiah added, "During the past six years, we have already begun reforms, but because of

112

continued disobedience to our Lord, fearful curses will fall upon us. Still if we return to the laws God gave us in this book, there is hope for our descendants and promise that our land will endure forever."

He gazed across the great gathering of his subjects. Then Enosh and his guards opened a passageway through the assembly to escort the king, the royal family, and all courtiers back to the palace. Walking tall and proud, Josiah nodded to the citizens. Shallum followed closely behind him.

A man standing near Huldah addressed another citizen. "I hope this great evil doesn't come during my lifetime."

"If King Josiah casts out every idol," the other replied, "maybe the evil won't come upon us at all."

A third man joined the conversation. "I'm going to follow the example of our king and worship only the Lord, the God of our fathers."

Murmuring in apprehension, the people began to leave the Temple area. Desperately trying to reach Shallum, Huldah pushed her way through the crowd. As men and women bumped into her, she realized that she could not possibly overtake her husband before he descended the steps into the king's garden.

There was only one way to find him. Ask Miriama for help. She turned and, shaking with impatience, continued with the crowd across the mount to the outer wall and then down the path that led through the small valley separating the hill from the city.

Sighing at their slow pace, she listened to women expressing their fear and men discussing the contents of the scroll. Only when they passed into the city streets was she able to quicken her steps. At last with the causeway to the palace ahead of her, Huldah broke into a run. At the outer gate the guards challenged her.

"Huldah, the prophetess and wife of Shallum, keeper of the king's wardrobe," she identified herself, fretting at the formality when the guards already knew her.

After again telling her name to the guards outside the women's garden, they admitted her. She ran along the path and asked the Nubians to open the door to the women's quarters. Inside she climbed the stairway to Jedidah's chambers and called, "Miriama, open for Huldah. Please hurry."

A maidservant swung open the door, and Huldah stumbled in. "Where's Miriama?"

Jedidah appeared at the door to her inner rooms. "Huldah! What is it?"

She took a deep breath and her words tumbled out. "Zophar has threatened Josiah and Shallum and me."

Jedidah came across the room and grabbed Huldah's hands. "We must warn Josiah and Shallum."

"Where's Miriama?" Huldah cried. "She could relay the message."

"She went home with her children." Jedidah's voice shook. "But it's no use to send a message. Josiah and Shallum aren't in the palace or the royal court."

"Not here!"

"No. To answer any questions the citizens might have, Josiah decided to tour the city. Shallum and Enosh and others went with him. They just now left the royal court."

Huldah let go of Jedidah's hands. "Then I will go."

"Where?"

"Into the city to look for them."

"You'll need help." Jedidah glanced at the maid standing near the windows. "I'll send some of my servants with you."

Huldah stepped away from her friend. "No! They

114

would just slow me down." She pulled open the door and hurried away.

* * *

In Jerusalem most of the women had returned to their homes, but men roamed through the streets, talking with their neighbors, questioning anyone they met about the message their king had read to them. Vendors set up a lively business as the men bought food and drink to quench their anxiety.

"Where's King Josiah now?" Huldah asked a shopkeeper.

He pointed down the street. "I'm told he's near the scribes' quarters."

Making her way along the narrow streets, she turned a corner and came upon a familiar figure standing outside the scribes' quarters. "Father!"

Barak frowned at her. "Daughter, what are you doing alone in the streets? The way these citizens are drinking, riots could result. Some are even resenting your interpretation of the writings in the scroll. Why haven't you gone home?"

Quickly she related what Zophar had said.

Her father took hold of her arm. "I'm escorting you to your house where you'll be safe. That's where you belong."

"But Shallum and Josiah. Someone has to tell them."

"Soldiers are with them. No one is going to attack Shallum or Josiah today."

Suddenly all her energy drained away, and Huldah allowed Barak to take her home. After he left, she wandered around her courtyard, unable to concentrate on anything except the thought, *When will Shallum come? Will I be able to warn him soon enough?* Finally with the dog Yaphe at her feet, she sat on a bench and quietly listened for her husband's footsteps. But the only sounds were a sparrow chirping to defend its territory and the cooks in the kitchen starting to prepare the evening meal.

The blue of the clear sky grew darker. The two men who served as night guards arrived to take up their post outside the gate. Huldah heard them conversing in low tones. The first star showed faint light, and still Shallum didn't come. A maidservant lit the courtyard torches. Shallum's menservants returned from the streets.

"Have you seen the master of this household," Huldah asked them. They shrugged their shoulders and shook their heads. As she forced herself to her room for a heavier shawl to ward off the cool night air, the gatekeeper announced, "Master Shallum is coming."

With Yaphe prancing beside her, Huldah ran across the courtyard to her husband. "I've been worried."

He held her in his arms and stroked her back. "The people asked many questions, and Josiah refused to leave until he had answered every one. But why were your worried? You knew I was with Josiah."

"On the Temple mount Zophar talked to me."

"What did he say?"

Huldah pressed her face against his shoulder and sobbed, "He threatened dire consequences for Josiah and for us if you and I don't give up our positions."

"That scoundrel," Shallum growled. "He has no right to threaten us."

The gate guards sounded an alarm. "Men are entering our street."

"Zophar," Huldah gasped.

She heard the challenge of the guards, "What are your intentions?" And then there were groans, then smashing blows sounded against the heavy sycamore door that served as the gate.

"Hide in the storeroom." Shallum pressed her toward it. "And take Yaphe with you." Dashing to his room, he grabbed swords for himself and his menservants, but before he could mobilize for resistance, 10 attackers had broken in and were upon him and his servants.

At the storeroom door, Huldah turned around. The dog barked vigorously and sprang toward the struggling men. Instinctively Huldah ran to her husband and pulled on the arm of the man beating him. He shoved her until she sprawled onto the hard courtyard stones. Yaphe grabbed the attacker's arm in his strong teeth. Cursing, the man kicked the dog, sending him reeling onto the stones.

By the time Huldah was able to lift her head, the men had already dragged Shallum out the gate and down the street. She looked around for help. The two menservants and the doorkeeper lay nearby. "Go after them," she screamed. One of them groaned. She crawled to him and discovered blood covering his face.

Rising to her feet, she looked outside the gate. Yaphe was nowhere to be seen. The guards lay stretched across the doorway. "Zophar and his men," one of them said weakly. "There were too many of them for us."

Huldah stumbled to the kitchen and found the cooks huddled in a corner. "Get the maids to help you bind up the men's wounds," she told them. Returning to the courtyard she called, "Yaphe!" He ran in from the street. "Go to Shallum," she ordered. The dog sniffed at the stones and darted through the open gate.

"Wait!" she called. "Wait for me."

Dutifully, as Shallum had trained him, he sat down until she caught up with him. Sniffing again, he headed toward the city's northern gate.

Oh, no, Huldah thought. *Yaphe expects me to take him for a run in the Kidron Valley and up the mount*. But then in the moonlight she saw him stop and sniff again at the stones before he bounded away, this time toward the city center. She breathed more easily. He was leading her toward the marketplace, where night watchmen outside the shops could tell her what they saw when Zophar and his men passed that way with Shallum.

But instead of continuing toward the marketplace, the dog circled around it. Suddenly he stopped. In a dark doorway a beggar lay sleeping. When Yaphe gave a sharp bark, the man reared up and held his hands in front of him. "Call off your dog."

"He won't harm you. But tell me, have you seen a group of men pass this way?"

"Men come and men go. Some return home very late this night."

Realizing she could gain no help from this beggar, she ordered the dog, "Go to Shallum." On they went through the dark streets. If only she could find a patrol of the king's soldiers, she could try to convince them that she needed help.

A stray cat scurried out of the way, and momentarily Yaphe darted after it. A rat sat atop a homeowner's wall and stared down at Huldah and her dog. Leaning against the wall, two men held flasks of strong drink. She could smell where they had spilled some on their robes. "Aha! A woman. Come join us pretty lady." One held out his flask to her.

Yaphe growled and Huldah asked, "Have you seen men pass this way?"

"Men? Ha. We've seen men pass this way and that way and every way. Now we've even seen a woman and a dog pass this way."

"Go home before you fall down," she muttered in exasperation.

Soon afterward as she turned a corner in the street, Yaphe lay down at her feet and released a low growl. Ahead of them the city wall formed a high barrier. A tall, stone tower rose in threatening reinforcement, and the gate was securely barred.

She held her hands against her chest to control her labored breathing. If Zophar had taken Shallum outside the wall, how could she and the dog leave? Even though they might let men go outside the city at night, would the guards allow a woman to leave?

She stooped to rub Yaphe's back, gaining comfort from his presence.

From the shadow of the tower a harsh voice rang out. "Who are you, and why are you at Valley Gate this time of night?"

Chapter 14

Lord, *keep my voice from trembling*, Huldah prayed silently. She stood up and drew in a deep breath. "I am Huldah, the prophetess, wife of Shallum, keeper of the king's wardrobe."

Two men emerged from the shadow. "If you're really Huldah, wife of Shallum, explain why you are at Valley Gate instead of in his home this time of night."

Yaphe snarled, and the men drew their swords. Huldah leaned down, putting her hand on the dog's neck to restrain him. "Please help me. Evil men attacked my husband. I believe they have taken him outside the city wall. I beg you to send a message to the king that his servant Shallum is in danger." She stood up. "I also beseech you to show your mercy and let me pass through this gate."

Still watching the dog, the men conferred until one announced, "We've come to a decision." He let out a taunting laugh. "We'll allow you to pass so you can see for yourself what's happening in the Hinnom Valley. Wait where you are until we open the gate." They backed away until they stood at the heavily-armored barrier.

Huldah's heart pounded in fearful suspicion. Were these some of Zophar's men posing as Josiah's soldiers? They unbarred the gate. "Pass."

Glancing anxiously from side to side, she hurried through with Yaphe slinking along at her side. The heavy doors clanked behind them. Moonlight revealed a path that descended the valley's steep side. Huldah hunched her shoulders to keep from trembling. The dreaded Hinnom, where Manasseh had sacrificed his children in the fires of Molech! No one wanted to come here even in the daytime. She had never heard of anyone venturing into the Hinnom at night.

The dog sniffed at the rocky ground and gazed up at his mistress. "Go to Shallum," she commanded. They progressed slowly. Huldah stopped often, watching for any sign of movement. A few scrubby cypress trees grew on the valley floor. Men could hide behind them. Part way down, the path turned and ran along the Hinnom's side. Yaphe halted abruptly. Looking upward he growled deep in his throat. High on the opposite side of the valley a pack of wild dogs were dark silhouettes against the sky.

While she waited for her dog to continue along the path, Huldah surveyed the scene below her. "Oh!" she gasped. A group of silent men were lifting a tightly bound figure onto a pile of stones. In the moonlight, Huldah could distinguish Shallum's striped robe. The man on the stone altar was her husband! She held her fist against her lips to stifle the scream that threatened to escape.

"I must do something to help him," she whispered. "But what?" Even if she were able to roll large stones down the hillside, they might hit Shallum instead of his assailants.

Yaphe, watching the dogs, raised his head and gave a howl, long and passionate. The pack answered with soaring howls that sent a shiver through Huldah's body.

The men's attention shifted from their grim task to the opposite side of the valley, where the dogs milled restlessly on the ridge top.

"Go to Shallum," Huldah ordered.

Continuing to bark loudly, Yaphe bounded forward. Excitement carried to the pack, and they leaped down the hillside to join him in a noisy race.

"Dogs!" shouted Zophar. "Wild dogs." He and his henchmen scattered, all running in the direction of the Kidron Valley. The dogs turned and pursued them, nipping at their heels, biting at their legs.

Huldah scrambled down the hillside to her husband. A container of bright coals lay on the ground—hot coals for lighting the altar fire. Moonlight gleamed off a knife that one of the men had dropped—perhaps the very knife he had intended to use on Shallum. She picked it up and quickly cut the cloth that gagged his mouth.

"Huldah, Huldah," he breathed her name. She sawed at the cords that bound his wrists and then worked on the cords around his ankles. Shallum tried to stand up, but stumbled and fell to the ground.

Huldah raised her head, listening to shouts that came from the direction of the Kidron. Yaphe trotted back from the pursuit. He lay down and licked his master's face. Then the dog stood up and looked toward the opposite side of the valley. When Huldah followed his gaze, she groaned, "Oh, no. All the dogs have given up the chase, and they're returning to the ridge."

Shallum pressed his ear to the ground. "I hear footsteps of men coming this way."

Zophar's men returning! She pulled on her husband's

arm. "Hold onto me, and I'll try to pull you up."

He tried to stand but was unable. "You go, Huldah. Go while there's still time."

"No. I'll not leave you here to die at the hands of Zophar." She peered into the shadows, searching for the men whom Shallum heard approaching. A cloud had drifted across the moon, making it difficult for her to see. Was someone moving behind those small cypress trees, or was it only her imagination? If Zophar was returning, how many men were with him?

The pounding of running feet echoed into her ears, and then Zophar's voice sliced through the night air. "I decided not to wait until this woman stopped prophesying. The time has come for both of you to die." In the moonlight, she could see the sword raised high above his head. Behind him, his henchmen drew their weapons.

Struggling to stand, Shallum was able to rise only to his knees.

Huldah stepped forward to face Zophar. "That will not happen."

"Is this one of your prophecies?" he sneered.

How can I divert him, confuse him? The words of Isaiah! "The Lord goes forth like a mighty man, like a man of war He stirs up His fury," she screamed at Zophar. "He cries out, He shouts aloud, He shows himself mighty against His foes."

Zophar laughed derisively. Slight movements in the valley behind him and his men caught Huldah's attention. Dark figures were creeping forward among the cypress. Were they some of the king's soldiers or more of this traitor's followers? "Do not forsake us, O Lord," she prayed quietly. "Make haste to help us."

Suddenly Yaphe jumped forward, baring his sharp

teeth, growling wildly. Zophar and his men backed away from the dog.

"Thus says the Lord. They shall be turned back and utterly put to shame, who trust in graven images, who say to molten images, 'You are our gods.' " She glared at the men facing her. "These words that Isaiah recorded are the Lord's Scripture, holy and true."

A trumpet blared. Yelling an ancient war cry, the king's soldiers sped forward. Zophar and his followers raised their swords, but the soldiers knocked their weapons to the ground. In a few minutes, Josiah's men had bound the traitors' hands and tied ropes around their necks.

At the sight of the king among the soldiers, Shallum called out, "Praise God!"

Josiah rushed to the man on the ground and with a mighty heave pulled him to his feet. "I'm thankful we arrived in time."

More soldiers poured from Valley Gate. Enosh was leading them. He scrambled down the hillside to report to the king. "We have arrested the band of Zophar's followers who had overcome your soldiers at Valley Gate, and now your patrols are searching the city for more."

"Good work," said Josiah. "Tonight these traitors will sit in the dungeon. Tomorrow I'll banish them to the southern wilderness."

Zophar let out a loud wail. "Banish!" he protested. "I do not deserve banishment to the wilderness."

Josiah scowled at him. "A large guard of soldiers on horseback will escort you and all your men, on foot and in chains, to the desert. There they will leave you in the territory of the nomadic tribes." He motioned to Enosh. "Take these vipers to the dungeon."

Exhausted, Huldah stepped closer to her husband.

When he put his arm around her, his warmth gave her renewed strength.

Josiah turned toward them, and his voice shook with emotion. "Huldah, you have once again proven your wisdom. When my soldiers saw a group of men still in the streets, they thought nothing of it. But when a lone woman and a dog appeared, they notified the palace."

"But I found none of your soldiers in the streets," Huldah protested. "How did they see me and my dog?"

"You thought you talked to a beggar and two drunken citizens, but they were really some of my spies. Others that you didn't see waited nearby." Josiah faced Shallum. "You have a brave wife, and I value her. She's a second mother to me, and you are the father I longed to have. To honor both of you, when I have another son, I will give him the name *Shallum*."

Tears of joy flooded Huldah's eyes. "At last we will have a grandson."

"Yes," agreed Josiah as he faced the city wall. "Now let's leave the Hinnom and the sadness of this valley where too many children have burned in the fires of Molech." He preceded them up the path toward the gate.

Supporting each other, Shallum and Huldah followed. Yaphe and a guard of soldiers walked behind them.

A faint glow of dawn tinted the eastern hills. Huldah looked toward the light. "Josiah will continue with his reforms, and the writers of our chronicles will record that he was a good king, that he did what was right in the sight of the Lord as his forefather David did. His descendants will include kings, even a King of kings."

They climbed out of the Hinnom, the valley of death, and entered Jerusalem, the city of life.